They moved together like they were old dance partners, gliding and swaying to Clint's tune, until the music stopped.

Susan opened her eyes and looked up at Clint. He had a peculiar smile on his face. She didn't see it coming until she felt his body tense.

He wouldn't.

He couldn't.

He did.

He bent her back and dipped her.

She felt herself flying through the air backward and gripped his arms like a lobster clutching his dinner. He had tight muscles and strong arms under his long-sleeved shirt, but she'd break both of them if he let her fall onto the barn floor.

He held her as he studied her face, as if debating whether or not to kiss her.

She held her breath. She wouldn't object....

Dear Reader,

I love writing about cowboys. They are tough, rugged and hard workers.

Well, maybe not all of them....

In *The Cowboy and the CEO* Wyoming native and bullfighter Clint Scully prefers to let his money work for him. He's invested wisely. That's why he just can't understand Susan Collins, who owns her own clothing company in New York City. She is one woman who needs to learn how to stop and smell the roses—and he's just the man to show her how.

I'm from upstate New York and recently took a trip to Manhattan to watch the Professional Bull Riders at Madison Square Garden. What a thrill! To see the cowboys walking around New York City in their gear was a contrast of lifestyles—just like the one Clint and Susan experience.

So sit back and put your boots up as I tell you a story about a bullfighter, a businesswoman and the little girl who brings them together.

Happy reading!

Christine Wenger

THE COWBOY
AND THE CEO

CHRISTINE WENGER

Silhouette

SPECIAL EDITION

Published by Silhouette Books

America's Publisher of Contemporary Romance

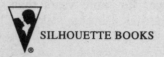

SILHOUETTE BOOKS

ISBN-13: 978-0-373-24846-9
ISBN-10:   0-373-24846-6

THE COWBOY AND THE CEO

Copyright © 2007 by Christine Wenger

Visit Silhouette Books at www.eHarlequin.com

Printed in U.S.A.

Books by Christine Wenger

Silhouette Special Edition

The Cowboy Way #1662
Not Your Average Cowboy #1788
The Cowboy and the CEO #1846

CHRISTINE WENGER

has been a probation officer for more years than she cares to remember. She has a master's degree in probation and parole studies and sociology from Fordham University. However, when she read her first romance novel, it was a life-changing experience, and she began writing romances in her spare time. A native central New Yorker, she enjoys watching professional bull riding and rodeo with her favorite cowboy, her husband, Jim.

Chris would love to hear from readers. She can be reached by mail at P.O. Box 1212, Cicero, NY 13039 or through her Web site at christinewenger.com.

To the bull riders who chase their dream
and to the bullfighters who protect them in the arena.
Please be careful!

A heartfelt thanks to Silhouette editors
Leslie Wainger, Susan Litman
Gail Chasan and Paula Eykelhof,
who made this writer's dream come true.

Chapter One

"I can't spare the time to fly to Wyoming," Susan Collins said to her administrative assistant, Bev Irwin. Susan held up the clipboard that was packed with papers. "Many of these orders require my personal attention."

"It's nothing that we can't take care of." Bev shook her head. "You haven't had any kind of vacation in ages. This would be a good compromise. You can fly to the Gold Buckle Ranch, enjoy their new spa and do a little business."

Susan didn't even look at the pamphlet Bev shoved in her hand, and began to pace. "Look, Bev, I appreciate your concern, but I have a business to run. I'll send one of our salespeople to the Gold Buckle to handle whatever Emily Dixon needs in sportswear for the campers. I'll only charge her half of our cost, or I'll donate whatever she wants. Anything for the kids."

"Mrs. Dixon didn't ask for any donations. All she asked for was you," Bev insisted. "She's heard of the fund-raising you've done for physically challenged children, and wants to see what you can do for her program."

That was flattering, but she didn't raise the money for any accolades. She did it in memory of her sister, Elaine. The money went for research, for any special equipment the kids might need, for tutors and books while they were in the hospital, and for fun. All children needed to have fun. She could help a little with the fund-raising, but she didn't have time for more.

Susan sighed. Surely whatever the owner of the Gold Buckle Ranch wanted could be done by phone, fax and e-mail. She flipped through the papers on her clipboard and paced. Where was the order for uniforms from that high school marching band?

Bev handed Susan another colorful pamphlet. "You're exhausted and you know it. You need a change of scenery, Susan. You need to *relax*. Besides, Emily Dixon seems like the nicest lady. You'd love her."

"How on earth did she hear about me out in Wyoming?" Susan asked, stopping her pacing long enough to lean against her desk.

Bev smiled. "Mrs. Dixon also liked the fact that your company is called Winners Wear. And she loved our motto—For Those Who Try Their Best. She said that's the very philosophy of the Gold Buckle Ranch. They try to reinforce the same goal to each of their campers—to do their personal best in spite of their handicap. Isn't that terrific?"

Susan nodded. Clearly, Emily Dixon got it.

Bev slid an unopened brochure across Susan's desk and began to unfold it. "You should see all the programs they have for children with different disabilities—Wheelchair Rodeo, the Gold Buckle Gang, Cowboy Quest for emotionally troubled kids who are facing legal troubles…"

Susan barely listened to the litany of programs. She didn't want to turn Mrs. Dixon down, but she had plenty of competent salespeople who could handle this project.

As she looked at her to do list on the clipboard, the page began to blur. Her eyes were tired, scratchy, and she was having a hard time focusing. She didn't panic. Small things. Easily correctible with a squirt of eye drops and another cup of high-octane coffee.

Bev continued to push. "Why can't you just

let your very talented staff do their thing and take a break?"

Because Winners Wear was *her* company, and she had to be involved in every detail, that's why.

But maybe Bev was right.

Bev snapped her fingers. "Uh-oh. None of the other salespeople are free to go to Wyoming. They'll be at the big trade show in Orlando that week."

The twitch under Susan's eye returned. "I forgot about the trade show."

"Susan…" Bev took a deep breath and held up the brochure. "Emily wants you to experience the essence of the ranch so you can develop a meaningful logo. She also wants cowboy-style shirts and jeans to give to the campers for each program. Then she'd like all kinds of other gear to stock a little camp store. She thinks it'll be a good fund-raiser and that the parents, caregivers and all their donors would want to buy that kind of merchandise."

Susan rubbed her forehead, feeling the start of a headache. She liked the fact that Emily Dixon chose her company, and *really* liked the fact that Emily was so dedicated to helping children.

Her sister, Elaine, would have loved to spend time at a place like the Gold Buckle Ranch.

Susan stood and leafed through the clipboard again, not remembering what she was looking for. "A week is too long."

Truthfully, she *was* exhausted. If she had enough energy to stand at the window and look down at the street, she'd see people pushing clothes racks from building to building. Vendors would be hawking goods from tables on the sidewalks, and shoppers looking for bargains would be haggling with them for better deals.

There was no place like New York's Garment District, and Susan loved the hustle and bustle and the energy of it all.

She'd started Winners Wear seven years ago, after her mother died. She'd bought this century old building with the money her mother had left her, her entire savings and a huge bank loan. Then she'd hired the best employees she could find, mostly eager young graduates from the city's fashion and design schools.

It had been a big gamble for her financially, but her sales staff started bringing in contracts—*big contracts*—immediately.

For most of the past seven years, she'd felt overwhelmed, but it had paid off. She worked hard, but she couldn't take all the credit. Everyone worked hard.

She hated to admit how tired she was. She couldn't do her best when she felt like a pile of scrap material.

Maybe she *should* go to Wyoming.

"Go and breathe some clean mountain air, boss," Bev said. "You'll come back nice and refreshed and raring to go. Don't worry about a thing here. We'll take care of everything while you're gone."

Susan took in a deep breath and let it out. Maybe it would be a good idea—before she ended up in the hospital herself.

No thanks. She'd had enough of hospitals when her sister was alive.

"Okay. I'll go," Susan mumbled. "Not for a week, though. I'll leave this Thursday and return on Saturday. Then I have to get back here and take care of business."

Clint Scully meandered through the parking lot toward the front doors of the Mountain Springs Airport. Every now and then, he'd slow his pace even more and take a gulp of strong, black coffee from a white take-out cup.

Nothing like a perfect Wyoming day. Not too hot. Not too cold. A warm breeze and a lot of sunshine. A perfect July day to drag out a lawn chair and take a snooze in the sun. He yawned in anticipation of doing just that.

Mrs. D had promised to bake him a blueberry pie if he picked up Susan Collins at the airport. His buddy Jake Dixon had warned him about his mother's matchmaking tendencies and reminded Clint that she'd sent Jake to pick up Beth Conroy, who became Mrs. Jake Dixon, just last year.

Clint swore under his breath. If Mrs. D had any ideas about matching him up with Susan Collins, she might as well spit in the wind.

Been there. Done that. He liked his freedom too much to commit to anyone.

Once inside the terminal, he checked the monitor and saw that Susan's plane had landed a few minutes ago, so he headed for baggage claim.

"Anyone here from the Gold Buckle Ranch?"

He looked around to see who was speaking, and his gaze landed on the prettiest woman he'd ever seen. She was tall, slender and buzzing from person-to-person like a bee in a flower bed.

Clint grinned. That *had* to be Susan Collins.

Her red-brown hair was done up in some kind of fancy braid. Her dark eyelashes fanned out on her cheeks like paintbrushes. She was as pale as an Easter lily—she looked as though she hadn't seen the warm kiss of the sun in years. She had on some kind of black jeans—designer jeans. A red blouse with a vee-neckline worked for her. The vee wasn't very plunging—just deep enough to make things interesting. Strappy black sandals with a slight heel made her legs look long and slender.

He stifled a wolf whistle and approached her.

Clint tweaked the brim of his hat. "I'm Clint Scully from the Gold Buckle." He stared into magnificent purple eyes. They must be colored contact lenses, he decided. No one had eyes like that. "And you must be…?"

"Susan Collins." She held out her hand, giving him a strong handshake. "Are you here to drive me to the ranch?"

He enjoyed warmth of her touch and the sureness of her handshake. "At your service."

"Thank you." She studied her luggage. "Where's the skycap for these bags?"

"I can get them. There's only two," he said, flexing.

"Oh, no. They are terribly heavy, especially that one." She pointed to the bigger black suitcase. "It's stuffed with samples and a couple of my catalogs."

"No problem," Clint said, lifting up the suitcases. Damn, they *were* heavy. What else had she brought from New York, the Statue of Liberty?

He managed a smile instead of a groan.

"No problem, darlin'. No problem t'all." He laid on the Texas accent. Ladies from the East usually loved his drawl.

"My name is Susan," she snapped. "And they wheel."

Mmm… Seemed like she wasn't the Texas-drawl type.

"Right this way, Susan. My truck's out front."

He wheeled her luggage and tried to keep up with her pace. She was walking fast, like she was late for a meeting or something.

"I'd like to get a massage after that dreadful flight," she said. "I'm *really* looking forward to the spa."

The words came out in a rush. She walked fast. She talked fast.

"The spa hasn't been inspected yet. Should be soon, though."

"Inspected?" she asked.

"A father of one of our campers donated the hot tub to the ranch. He said that it'd be good relaxation for the caretakers of the children. Mr. D had it installed on the deck of the Caretaker Hotel by the baseball diamond."

She raised a perfect eyebrow. "A *hot tub?* But what about the spa? Massages? Facials? Wraps?"

He shook his head and looked confused. "Mrs. D is the only one who calls it a spa. Everyone else calls it a hot tub. I think there's a communication problem somewhere."

Susan closed her eyes. "I came all this way for a hot tub by a baseball diamond?" She sighed. "Wait until I tell Bev."

Clint told Susan to wait at the curb and went to get his truck. By the time he returned, three cowboys were talking to Susan—hitting on her, really. Bronc riders, he assumed, probably on their way to Cheyenne for the Frontier Days festivities. Bronc riders thought they were hot stuff.

"Toss those suitcases in the back, boys," Clint said, interrupting their conversation. They did so, and then went back to ogling Susan.

"Thanks for your help." He shook their hands, in an effort to send them on their way. "Goodbye now."

One of the cowboys pointed at him. "Hey, aren't you…?"

"Yeah," Clint said, always flattered by the recognition. "Yeah, I am."

Clint opened the door for Susan to get in.

"Just who do they think you are?" she asked.

"Just myself." He grinned. "They've probably seen me around—either fighting bulls or hauling my stock to rodeos."

"I see."

She gave a big sigh and checked her watch. She got into the truck, and so did he. He aimed the pickup toward the mountains.

"Mr. Scully, how long will it take to get to the ranch? I'd like to meet with Emily tonight and show her my samples."

"I don't think that'll be possible. Emily will be busy with the kids. Then after dinner, it's popcorn and movie night. We're showing one of the Harry Potter movies. You won't want to miss that."

"I didn't think that the program had started yet."

"This is Thursday. Right?"

Susan nodded.

"Our Wheelchair Rodeo program ends on Saturday morning, and the Gold Buckle Gang will be arriving on Saturday afternoon. It's a program for—"

"Kids who use crutches or braces," she said softly, pinching the area above her nose as if she were getting a headache.

"How did you know that?"

"I read it in the flyer," she said. "On the plane."

He wasn't sure if she was really interested in the Gold Buckle Gang program or if she was getting a headache. He narrowed his eyes as he watched her.

"Make sure you don't miss the big game on Sunday night. We use a beach ball and the batter uses a big plastic bat. We have shortened bases and the cowboys do some clowning around and get the kids laughing and—"

"Sounds like fun," she said. "But I'll probably be gone by then."

She sounded remote, disinterested. He wondered why. "It is fun, but it also serves a purpose.

The kids develop balance and maybe exercise different muscles, or maybe rely a little less on their crutches. Or maybe they just get to laugh a little more than usual." Clint grinned. "Wait until you see the horseshoe toss, and the relay races and some of the other events we have at the end of the program that make up the Gold Buckle Rodeo. We give out gold and silver buckles for the winners."

"Buckles?"

"It's a western thing. Rodeo winners have always received belt buckles—like this beauty." He gripped the big gold buckle he sported and tapped it. "National Championship Bullfighting—2006." He was proud of that, and he'd won the competition four times in a row. The competition was getting tougher and tougher every year, but he still had the moves.

He smiled at Susan. "Maybe we'll get you to play a little beach ball–baseball with the kids."

But he doubted she would. Miss New York City seemed to be even more distant.

"No. I can't," she said abruptly. "I didn't know that a program would be starting and the kids would be here. For some reason, I thought I'd be here in between programs." She took a deep breath and looked out the window. "Like I said, I'll be leaving on Saturday. I have to get back home."

She was getting downright frosty, but he still pushed. "Well, you'll be staying at least a couple days. You'll enjoy the ranch and the kids. The kids are the best."

She didn't answer, then sighed. "I'm suddenly very tired, Mr. Scully. It was a long flight."

Just before she turned her head to look out the side window, he could swear he saw moisture in her eyes. Now he felt bad.

"Susan, did I upset you somehow?"

"Oh, no. No. You didn't. Like I said, I'm just tired."

That was just an excuse. Something was wrong. She seemed really tense when he talked about the kids. Something was going on.

Clint concentrated on the road ahead, knowing that he'd somehow put a damper on Susan Collins's arrival in Wyoming.

He usually stayed far away from women like her— rich, successful, city women who had plenty of money but no heart. Women who were just like his former fiancée, Mary Alice Bonner. Hell, Susan looked like she could teach Mary Alice a few things.

But for some reason, he wanted to—needed to—see Susan Collins smile. He wanted to get her to relax, to get rid of the burden weighing her down.

And if anyone could do that, it was Clint Scully.

Chapter Two

Susan didn't want to get involved with the kids. She was afraid it would hurt too much.

She was just supposed to help design a logo and a line of merchandise for the ranch, and that was all she intended to do.

It wasn't that she didn't care. Quite the opposite. She hadn't been thinking clearly when she'd agreed to come here—she wasn't sure she could bear facing a group of children whose pain so reminded her of her beloved sister's.

To this day, she could remember the smells and sounds of the hospital where she visited Elaine, who'd died way too young.

As soon as Emily was available, she'd meet with her to discuss what Winners Wear could offer. Then she'd take her scheduled flight out of Mountain Springs on Saturday morning. Bev had bought her an open-ended airline ticket, thinking that she'd decide to stay and relax and enjoy the spa.

She'd be leaving in two days.

With that decided, she glanced at Clint to see if he was still alive. He walked slow. He talked slow. He even drove slow.

Anyone could see that on this wide-open road without a car or a cop in sight, he could go at least seventy.

She checked her watch. "Clint, how far away is the Gold Buckle?"

"A couple of hours."

"Oh."

He could easily cut that time in half if he'd just step on it. Then again, she doubted that the huge, rusty pickup could go much over the forty miles an hour at which he was currently cruising.

She stole another quick glance at Clint. She had to admit he was handsome in a rugged, outdoorsy way. He had a lazy, sexy smile with a little dimple at the corner of his mouth.

Clint Scully was intriguing.

Maybe it was because he was the first actual cowboy she'd ever met. Certainly, it wasn't because his jeans hugged his strong thighs, or because his legs were so long that he could barely fold them beneath the dash. Or the fact that he smelled like fresh air and warm cotton.

Her cheeks heated, and she rolled down the window a little more. She reached up and swept the hair that had escaped her French braid off the back of her neck, trying to catch some much-needed air.

She stole another glance at Clint and saw the laugh lines around his eyes. His hands were tanned and strong. She studied the sharp crease of his long-sleeved, blue-checkered shirt. His light brown hair stuck out from under his white cowboy hat and brushed the back of his shirt collar. Her eyes strayed farther south.

He sure did fill out those jeans.

"Something wrong?" he asked, glancing over at her and grinning.

"Um...no. Just admiring your truck."

That was a lame recovery, but she'd die of embarrassment if he ever guessed that she was checking him out. She decided to change the subject.

"Why did those cowboys at the airport know you?"

"They've probably seen me working the rodeo events. I'm a bullfighter. That's the new politically correct term for a rodeo clown."

"You mean you toss around a red cape and get the bull to charge you like they do in Spain?"

"Absolutely not." He chuckled. "You've never seen a rodeo or a bull riding event, have you?"

She shook her head. "Not once."

He whistled. "I thought everyone in North America had seen one at one time or another."

"Not everyone."

He made a sharp right turn onto a bumpy road. Susan gripped the lip of the dash so she wouldn't fall over onto him. She thought her teeth were going to rattle loose from her head.

"So what does a bullfighter do?" she asked.

"I protect the bull riders."

"From what?"

"From the bull."

"Just how do you do that?"

"Various techniques, but mostly I'm fast on my feet."

Her heart started to pound as she thought of a huge bull charging him or anyone else. "Are you crazy?"

"Mostly." He shrugged. "But then I think you're crazy for living in New York City, but to each his—or *her*—own." He paused for a bit then added, "Anyone special going to be missing you back in New York?"

Hmm… She didn't know whether or not she

liked the fact that he was asking about her availability. He was nothing like any man she'd ever met, and would be interesting to get to know, but that was all. She had no interest in a casual fling.

"If you're asking me if I'm married, I'm not. Marriage isn't for me. I don't have time for relationships. How about you? Anyone worried that you're going to kill yourself saving cowboys from bulls?"

"No. Marriage isn't for me, either. Most women aren't happy living down on the ranch once they've seen what the world has to offer."

"Sounds like you speak from personal experience."

There was silence. Then he raised a finger from his grip on the wheel and pointed at the horizon. "Bet you don't get sunsets like that back home."

The sun looked like a big red ball stuck between two peaks of lacy black mountains. Slivers of purple and yellow and red shot across the sky, and she wondered how long it had been since she'd taken the time to watch a sunset.

She knew the answer to that—not since she'd gotten too busy building her company.

"We might get sunsets like that," she said, "but there are too many buildings in the way for me to see it from my office or my apartment. Those who live on a high floor can see it."

"What a shame," Clint said, shaking his head. "So what do you do in New York?"

"I make uniforms and sportswear."

"Uniforms? What kind?"

"Everything from high school band to major league baseball and everything in between." She hesitated, and then said with pride, "I own my own company. I call it Winners Wear, and our motto is 'For Those Who Try Their Best.'"

"Nice." He nodded. "I like it. But running your own company seems like a lot of responsibility."

"It is. I really shouldn't have left New York. I have a million things that need tending to."

She fished around in her purse, pulled out her daily planner, slid out a gold pen and reviewed the list of items she needed to discuss with Mrs. Dixon.

She made notes until the light faded. "Could you turn on the overhead light?" she asked Clint.

"Sorry. It's broken. Why don't you sit back and enjoy what's left of the ride?"

She had no choice, now did she? She put her planner away and stared out the window.

They pulled into the Gold Buckle just after sundown. She couldn't see much of the grounds in the dusk, only the welcoming indoor lights of several small log cabins strung along a brook that glistened in the moonlight.

"This looks just like a real ranch," she said.

"It is a real ranch." Clint slowed down and made a right turn. "Mrs. D said to put you in the Homesteader Cabin and that she'll try to come by later to give you a proper welcome, along with something to eat. That all right with you?"

"Fine. Maybe we can have our meeting then."

"I thought you were tired."

"The sooner I meet with Emily, the sooner we can take care of business."

Clint pulled up in front of one of the log cabins, the second one from the end. In the glow of the porch light by the cabin door, Susan could see two rocking chairs. Large pine trees loomed behind the structure. If there were snow, it'd look like a Christmas card. She wondered if the guests in the other little cabins were at dinner or snuggled up inside.

Susan felt a little thrill of excitement zip through her when she caught the scent of horses on the breeze. She remembered the riding lessons she'd taken one summer in White Plains—a gift from her father when she was twelve. Her mother had protested, but her father had insisted.

"Susan needs to have some fun, Rochelle," he'd told her mother in one of his rare moments of strength. "And you know how much she loves horses. I'll take her on the train, wait for her and ride back with her."

Those were the best six Saturdays of her young life. After that, her father was gone again, escorting a tour group to Europe. He never managed to stay with them for very long.

Shaking off the sad thoughts, she gathered up her planner and her purse as Clint turned on the overhead light.

"Must be working after all," he said, giving her a wink.

He'd lied to her. The light never was broken. He'd just wanted her to look at the scenery. He'd manipulated her, and she didn't like that, but if he hadn't, she would have kept her face in her planner and missed the beauty of this country.

Clint got out of the truck. He walked her up the stairs of the cabin, his hand holding her elbow lightly. That was polite and gentlemanly of him. He opened the door with a large key and flicked on the light.

She glanced around the room and spotted a phone. "Can I make long-distance calls?"

"That phone only rings to the main office in case of emergency."

"I can't live without a phone. Thank goodness I have my cell." She flipped open her phone. "Why can't I get a signal?"

"It won't work around here. Too many mountains surrounding us. But Em and Dex have a phone in the office you can use." He gripped the door handle. "I'd better haul your luggage in."

"Where's the bell person?"

"I guess that'd be me. We all pitch in around here."

Susan turned around and found herself forehead-to-nose, toe-to-toe with Clint Scully. He grabbed her elbows to steady her.

His eyes studied her face, and then his gaze traveled down to her breasts. She probably should have been offended, but in truth she was flattered. It had been a long time since a man had looked at her that way. He seemed to see right through her, reaching down to a part of her that hadn't been touched in years. The same heat that had licked at her insides before flared again.

He cocked an eyebrow as if he was wondering what she'd do next.

She held her breath, wondering what he'd do.

It'd been a long time since she'd been with a man, and being so close to Clint reminded her of that fact.

She'd given up on men a while ago. They just couldn't understand that her company came before they did.

Yet Clint was very, very tempting, and very different. If his scorching gaze was any indication, he was as attracted to her as she was to him.

He gave his hat a tug. "I'll go get your luggage. Why don't you relax?"

"Thanks, Clint." She offered her hand, to shake his. "For everything."

He raised her hand an inch from his lips. "My pleasure, Susan."

Surely, he wouldn't... No one did that anymore.

Clint did. A whisper of warm air and soft lips brushed the back of her hand, and she melted like polyester under a too-hot iron.

Clint Scully was one interesting man.

Trying to gather her thoughts, she listened to the dull sound of his boots fade as he walked down the stairs of the porch. Then she explored the cabin.

The walls were tongue-and-groove knotty pine, varnished to a shine. Lace curtains on the window gave it a homey touch. Brightly striped Hudson's Bay blankets slashed bits of color around the cottage. It was open and airy with high ceilings and chunky log furniture with bright cushions in a Native American arrow design.

A huge stone fireplace took up most of one wall, and a pile of wood was stacked on a circular stand nearby. She looked for the switch that would make the fireplace spring to life.

"It's the real thing," Clint said, appearing next

to her with her luggage. "I'll show you how to start a fire if you'd like."

"I think I can figure it out."

She thought how nice it would be to sit before a real fire at night and read a book. She hadn't had time to read a book in ages. That was something else she'd been missing.

"I'll leave these here, then I'll see about getting your dinner," Clint said.

She walked him to the door and felt all warm and fuzzy when he tweaked his hat and disappeared into the dark night.

Susan Collins, CEO, hadn't felt warm and fuzzy since mohair was in fashion.

Clint grabbed a frosty cold bottle of Chardonnay from the fridge in his travel trailer and set it on the countertop. In three steps, he was inside his bathroom checking his appearance in the mirror above the sink.

Clint bought the thirty-foot trailer from Ronnie Boggs, a down-on-his-luck cowboy who was quitting bull riding. He remembered pulling out his wallet and handing Ronnie more than double his asking price. Ronnie refused to take all that, but Clint wouldn't take no for an answer and stuffed the money into the tough cowboy's pocket.

Clint towed it from event to event wherever he

was working. He liked the privacy and the quiet, and the fact that he could cook his own meals and relax in his own surroundings. Besides, if he stayed in a hotel, the riders would give him the business.

Whenever he was at the Gold Buckle Ranch, which was every summer and whenever else his pal Jake Dixon needed him, he parked it in his usual spot, deep in the woods behind the cabins. His favorite thing to do was to crank out the awning, sit in a lawn chair under it and listen to the brook as it sluiced over the rocks.

As Clint walked over to the boxes filled with jeans, shirts and work gear from his sponsors, he reminded himself to fire up his laptop and transfer funds. He'd heard on the stock contractors' grapevine that a couple of rank bulls might be going on auction with a starting bid of seventy-five thousand each. He'd been waiting and watching for those bulls and would pay any amount for them. They'd make a good addition to his stock.

He grabbed a new shirt from one of the cardboard boxes stacked in the corner. Pulling it out of the plastic wrap, he slid off the little white clips and shook out the shirt. Slipping it on, he could still see the fold marks. He puffed out his chest, and the creases faded. Well, he couldn't do that all night. He'd just have to hope for dim lighting.

He swung by the mess hall and collected a picnic basket loaded with food for Susan's dinner, and soon he was heading back to the Homesteader Cabin to see her again.

Ahh, Susan. She was so tense, so coiled up, she appeared to be about to spring. There was a sadness about her—he could see it in her deep purple eyes. Maybe he could distract her for a while.

He had a feeling that Susan Collins would dig her own subway back to New York when she looked out the window tomorrow morning and saw a couple hundred kids engaged in various activities. She didn't seem the kid type, but then again, he'd just met her. And he wanted to get to know her better.

Clint walked down the dimly lit path from the campgrounds that led to the cabins, a wine bottle gripped in one hand, the picnic basket that Cookie had given him for Susan swaying in the other.

He took the steps of the Homesteader Cabin two at a time and gave a light knock on the door.

"Who is it?" Her voice was slurred, sleepy.

"It's Clint. I brought your dinner."

"Just a minute."

She opened the door and Clint immediately liked what he saw. She'd changed into a dark pink golf shirt. On the pocket was bright embroidery in primary colors—her company logo, a halo of stars surrounding "Winners Wear." Printed underneath that, in bright orange, was her motto—For Those Who Try Their Best. Khaki pants clung to a great pair of hips. On her feet were fuzzy pink socks. Her auburn hair was in a ponytail high on her head, and a pair of gold-rimmed reading glasses were barely hanging on to the tip of her nose.

She held up the latest issue of *Pro Bull Rider Magazine*. "It was on the coffee table. Interesting sport, bull riding."

He set the picnic basket and wine down on the kitchen table. "You'll have to see it in person sometime."

She shook her head. "I don't know about that."

"I guarantee you'll love it."

"Care to wager that bottle of Chardonnay against that?"

He opened the picnic basket and pulled out several items wrapped in waxed paper. "You know, we've had a few bull riding events at Madison Square Garden."

"No kidding?"

"No kidding. Now, grab a chair and let's see what Cookie made for us." He opened one of the bigger packages. "Roast beef sandwiches."

He kept unwrapping and found pickles, a container of macaroni salad, two apples, potato chips and a couple of cans of cranberry-grape juice.

"Cookie thinks of everything," Clint said.

"What's his real name?"

"I don't know, actually. Every cook is called Cookie. It's a throwback to the chuck-wagon and trail-drive days." He held up the bottle of Chardonnay. "Some wine?"

"Why not?"

Clint opened the wine and found a couple of glasses in the cabinet next to the sink. Filling them halfway, he handed one to Susan. "Here's to your stay at the Gold Buckle Ranch."

"Thank you." They clinked glasses. "You like it here, don't you, Clint?"

"I do. I love the kids. They have a lot of heart and what we cowboys call *try*. The volunteers that come every year are special people, and the Dixons are the epitome of *try*. I see that you have the word in your logo."

"Emily liked my logo, too. That's why I'm here, I guess. But I can't take all the credit. My mother and I came up with our motto, theme, mission statement, whatever you want to call it when we were making nurses' uniforms in our kitchen. Trying our best is what got us through some tough years."

"And now you're the CEO of your own company." He shook his head. "That took a ton of 'try.'"

The way her eyes brightened and the way she

smiled, he could tell she was proud of herself. She should be. But there was still that haunting sadness in her eyes.

They ate and talked about nothing in particular and everything in general until he noticed that she was trying to stifle a yawn.

He was just about to leave when Mrs. D came up the steps of the Homesteader Cabin.

"I saw your light on, Susan, and I wanted to stop by and welcome you to the Gold Buckle Ranch," Emily said. "Evening, Clint. Did you see to our guest?"

"Yes, ma'am."

"I knew you would." She flashed him a teasing smile.

"Emily, do come in." Susan stood, looking for her sample books. "Would you like to talk about the merchandise now?"

"Heavens no, sweetie. It's late and you must be exhausted. I just wanted to welcome you and make sure you have everything you need."

Mrs. Dixon enveloped Susan in a big bear hug. Susan closed her eyes and looked uncomfortable at first, but Emily didn't let go. Eventually, Susan's tense expression turned into a big grin.

And Clint realized that Susan seemed to need just such a hug.

Emily was about Susan's height, and was one of those women who perpetually smiled. She wore her brown hair short, tucked behind her ears, and she seemed like a bundle of controlled energy.

Emily took a couple of steps into the Homesteader Cabin. "Maybe I will come in for a minute. It's been a stressful day—nothing big—just a bunch of little things."

"Anything I can help you with?" Clint asked.

Emily made her way to the living room and sat down on the couch, clearly exhausted. "I don't think so, Clint, but thanks, anyway. My biggest problem is that my arts and crafts teacher had to leave tonight. She was going to chaperone on the trail ride, too. Her daughter is having a baby, and it's coming earlier than they thought."

"I hope you find someone," Susan said.

"Me, too. I'd hate to cancel the arts and crafts program next week when the Gold Buckle Gang program begins. The kids just love making things and taking them home as presents."

"How about someone from town?" Clint asked.

"I've already put out feelers, but so far, there have been no calls, and I'm running out of time. Beth wanted to help—" She turned to Susan. "Beth's my daughter-in-law, Jake's wife. But she's due to deliver *her* baby in a couple of weeks, and the doctor wants her to stay off her feet."

Susan knew she should offer to help, but she'd be leaving in a couple of days herself. Besides, she truly didn't know if she could handle working with the kids in such close proximity.

She'd kept her charity work at a distance by donating money and by organizing and running fund-raisers. She did everything she could for handicapped children in Elaine's memory. But she had never worked with children on a one-on-one basis. She didn't think she'd ever be able to face that pain.

"Well, this is my problem," Emily said to Susan. "I didn't mean to burden you with it on your first night. You're here to relax and enjoy our spa. It should be operational soon. You're staying with us a week. Right, Susan?"

Susan bit back a smile at the spa reference. She now knew that it was a hot tub on a deck somewhere. "Don't worry about the spa. And, Emily, I'm sorry, but I'm only staying for a couple of days."

As he listened to the women chatting, an idea struck Clint—one that guaranteed him more time with Susan. Clint snapped his fingers. "Susan, why don't you take over the class. You'll be great. The kids will love you. Stay the week."

Emily smiled. "Oh, Susan, that would be wonderful! I don't think the classes would take up too much of your time. Just Monday through Friday—two hour-long classes a day."

Susan's mouth went dry, and she felt an uncomfortable lump in her stomach. She *had* to convince Emily that she wasn't staying for an entire week. That she'd planned on leaving the day after tomorrow.

"I don't know if I'd be that great with the kids," Susan finally said.

"Sure you would." Clint winked at her. "And I really love your company's motto—For Those Who Try Their Best." He raised an eyebrow, pointing to the logo on her shirt. He gave her the thumbs-up sign.

Oh, he was sneaky! She could see through him like cheap gauze. He had thrown her own motto back at her.

"Oh…Emily. Okay. I'll do it," she heard herself say. "For the whole week."

"You are a darling!" Emily gathered her into another big hug. "Thank you so much."

Thanks to Clint and his cute dimple and turquoise eyes, she'd just volunteered. To be a teacher. She didn't know how to teach. She didn't know anything about arts and crafts. She'd made a key chain out of braided boondoggle once, if that counted.

Emily walked to the door. "I'll rearrange my

schedule to give us some time to plan. Are you also willing to chaperone on the overnight campout and trail ride, too? If not, I understand. I'm already taking too much advantage of you."

She looked at Clint. "I-I'll do it."

What was she doing? The words were just coming out of her mouth. Maybe she was just overtired. She'd never acted like this.

"Susan, do you know how to ride?" Emily asked.

"Not really, but I took some lessons when I was twelve."

"Clint will refresh your memory. All of our horses are very gentle. And I promise that classes will only be for an hour or two each day. That'll leave you plenty of time for yourself."

Emily put an arm around Susan. "I can't thank you enough for volunteering. Now, you get some sleep. You've had a long day, and Clint will be here early to take you to breakfast at the dining hall and give you a riding lesson. Good night— to both of you."

With a wave, Emily was gone from the cabin.

Susan headed for the couch and sat down. She'd never backed down on a promise, and she didn't intend to start now.

Clint sat opposite her on the coffee table. "That was a really nice thing you did, volunteering to help Mrs. D."

"I think *you* were the one who volunteered me, Clint Scully. *My* volunteering would have made more sense if I knew something about arts and crafts and riding." She smiled to take some of the sting out of her voice.

"I believe you'll be a wonderful teacher." He stood and tweaked his hat.

She just loved it when he did that. And how could she be mad at him when his eyes sparkled like that?

She'd be mad enough later when she thought about it. Mad at herself. Clint had outwitted her, and it had been a long time since she'd had the rug pulled out from under her.

Maybe she really did want to stay.

Chapter Three

How could she even think such a thing?

Stay here? She'd been counting on doing business, with a relaxing spa weekend on the side—not playing teacher at a kids' camp. But here she was—trapped. And it was her own fault for volunteering.

"Susan, I'll help you with your classes anytime. Day or night," Clint said.

Now, that was a loaded statement. Clint was a flirt, and she was very rusty in the flirting department.

Standing, she walked to the door. Clint got the message and sauntered over to her. "I'll be sure to call on you if I need you," Susan said, then waited a few beats. "Day or night."

He grinned. Tweaked his hat. "See you in the morning."

She could hear the thud of his boots as he walked onto the porch and down the stairs. She locked the door behind him, then sat down on the couch.

She had to think of something besides Clint. The cowboy was getting under her skin, making her stomach flutter and her heart do little flips in her chest. For heaven's sake, she was a business-woman, not a freshman in high school.

Don't think about him. Think about your class.

She'd just promised Emily that she'd teach arts and crafts, but she didn't have a clue as to how to begin. Or even how to relate to the campers.

She'd never been a child herself.

But she never broke her word, not where kids were concerned. She'd been just about to tell Emily that she was only good at writing checks, when the "I'll do it" had come rocketing out of her mouth—not once, but twice.

So she'd try to make her arts and crafts program a success. She would develop it like a business project with a workable plan, realistic goals; set some milestones and plot it all out.

With that decided, she walked over to the refrigerator, suddenly dying for a hearty gulp of leftover Chardonnay.

Her reflection in the window caught her by surprise. It was so dark outside. No streetlights, no marquees, no car lights or skyscrapers lit for night. No TV. No radio. Just darkness and silence. With this kind of peace and quiet, she'd die of boredom within fifteen minutes.

Unless she had a certain cowboy to amuse her.

Reaching in her purse, she took out her cell phone to call Bev at home and check on things at Winnoro Wear, but then she remembered the time difference. Bev was probably fast asleep. Checking her cell, she saw there was still no signal. With a sigh, she tossed the cell phone back into her purse.

She paced. She sipped some wine. She paced some more. Sipped. Paced. Sipped. Paced. Sipped.

Finally, she decided that she should try to get some sleep. Maybe in the light of day, she'd find her lost mind.

She checked to make sure the door was locked, then for a little extra security, she pushed a heavy chair against the door. She missed her myriad locks, dead bolts and chains.

Back in the bedroom, she changed into a pair of sweatpants and a long white T-shirt, and eyed the puffy comforter on the bed. Slipping inside the covers, she sighed as the delicious warmth enfolded her. The bed was perfect. Now for some sleep.

She turned the light off and couldn't believe how dark and quiet it actually was.

There was no glare from the streetlights. No angry blare of car horns or revving motors. No shouting.

How did people live like this?

Staring up at the ceiling, eyes wide open, she tried to will herself to sleep, but Clint Scully kept intruding on her thoughts.

Cowboy. Handsome. Turquoise eyes. Boots. Sideways smile. Little dimple on the side of his mouth. Excellent butt.

She smiled and snuggled deeper into the bed when she heard a fluttering noise and felt the slightest breeze against her face.

"What?"

She thought that maybe the noise was a squirrel on the roof of the cottage. Did squirrels come out at night? What if it was a mountain lion or something with lots of sharp teeth? After all, this was the wilderness.

Something fluttered. And then again. Whatever it was, it was in her room.

Holding her breath, she flicked on the light and picked up her purse for protection.

A black bird flew by.

No. A bat!

She screamed. It flew by her face. She screamed again. Then again for good measure.

She sprang out of bed and tried to remember what she knew about bats.

Absolutely nothing.

She swung at the thing with her purse, ducking and dodging. The bat flew into the living room. On shaky legs, she turned on every light that she could find.

She screamed and swung again as it flew by her. She heard a series of knocks at the door or perhaps it was her heart pounding against her chest.

"Susan? It's Clint. Susan, are you all right?"

What a stupid question. "No, I'm not all right. There's a bat in here!"

The door rattled. "I can't get in."

On wobbly legs, she managed to run over and unlock the door so Clint could squeeze in.

"Where is it?"

"Over by the fireplace."

Clint squinted. "That little thing?"

"It's a bat! Do something!"

"I will."

He moved her away from the door. The bat flew out. He closed the door. "Gone."

Her head became a little woozy and she couldn't stop herself from swaying forward.

Then the shock of something cold and wet splashed on her face brought her around.

She gasped. "W-what are you doing?"

"There was a glass of water on the table, and I—"

"I know what you did, but that was wine."

Clint grinned. His eyes didn't move to meet hers, but were riveted to her chest.

She looked down. The wine had made the fabric of the white T-shirt cling to her breasts.

She rolled her eyes and plucked the material away from her body.

"Thank you for getting rid of the bat. Good night."

She stood up to reach for a blanket, but her knees wouldn't hold her yet. Just before they gave out completely, Clint caught her.

She let him hold her, enjoying how his hands roamed over her back and how warm his chest felt against her wet breasts. How his hard body felt against her.

Suddenly nervous, she stepped back, grabbed a blanket and wrapped it around herself. Disappointment dimmed his eyes.

"How did you happen to be here?" she asked.

"I walked Mrs. D home and was just going back to my trailer when I heard you scream. Actually, I think they heard you up in Canada."

She laughed. "Thanks, Clint. I'm glad you were here. I'll be okay now."

"Do you want me to stay with you? I'll take the couch."

Actually, she did want him to stay, but she just couldn't deal with knowing that Clint was in her cabin. She'd never sleep.

"No, thanks. I'm just going to sleep with all the lights on. It'll make it feel more like home."

He grinned. "Suit yourself."

He walked to the door, opened it, locked it again, and the cowboy disappeared into the dark Wyoming night.

The next morning, Susan awoke with the sun shining through the lace curtains. She swore she could see her breath in the frigid cabin.

She pulled the quilt off the bed and wrapped it around herself. Then she searched the bedroom for a thermostat so she could turn up the heat, but there was none to be found.

From habit, she slipped on her watch and checked the time. Eight o'clock. She hadn't slept this long in years. If she'd been home, she would have already put in about two hours at work.

She'd slept so soundly. Maybe there was something to this "clean mountain air" thing after all.

She tightened the comforter around herself,

yanked on her fuzzy pink socks and walked into the living room.

She found the thermostat next to the fireplace, set it at seventy degrees and sat on the sofa, tucking her feet under her to warm them. It felt like December in New York instead of July in Wyoming.

She looked out the window in front of her and saw a kid go by on a horse. He had braces on both legs, and he was grinning and looking around as he rode, like a king surveying his realm. A cowboy walked beside the big horse, and her heart did a funny leap in her chest, thinking of Clint.

Control yourself, Susan.

She heard footsteps on the porch and soon heard a knock on her door.

"It's Clint."

In spite of trying to be in control, she felt her heart do a funny leap anyway. "Come in," she said. She knew he had a key.

The door opened, flooding the room in sunlight. She squinted at Clint.

"It's colder in here than it is outside. Why didn't you open the windows?"

"I never thought of that. That's not the usual way it works."

"That's the way it works around here."

He walked around the cottage and opened the

windows. Sunlight and warmth filled the room. She loosened the comforter. He was right. It was warmer outside.

Clint sat opposite her on a big leather chair and propped an ankle on his knee. "How'd you sleep after the bat?"

"Like a rock. I put the covers over my head and didn't move a muscle."

"Did you forget that we have a breakfast date?"

He studied her with a grin, and she knew she must look a sight. How come he looked so good in the morning? Judging by the crease marks on his long-sleeved pink shirt, it looked like he'd just taken it out of a package. His jeans were dark denim and also looked new, and he sported a belt buckle the size of a saucer.

He looked bright and chipper, and she felt as if she'd been run over by a double-decker tour bus. Life just wasn't fair.

"And don't forget your riding lesson," he said. "I only have one day to make a cowgirl out of you."

She hadn't forgotten, but hoped he had.

"Let's get moving—we've got a long day."

What happened to the check-his-pulse, laid-back cowboy from yesterday?

"Is there coffee in the dining hall?" she asked.

"Buckets of it."

"I'll be ready in ten minutes," she said, springing up from the couch and running to the shower.

She figured she'd just get some coffee to go and maybe a bagel with cream cheese. Her stomach was jittery enough from the bat last night and now she had to get up on a horse and try to ride? It'd been *years* since she'd been on horseback.

When she was ready, Clint opened the door for her and she stepped out into the bright sun. Halfway down the path and aiming for the biggest building, she heard a shrill whistle.

Looking around she realized that Clint hadn't budged from the porch of her cottage. "Something wrong?" she asked.

"I always like the view from here."

Curious, she walked back toward the porch and stood a few feet away from him, following his gaze to the mountains in the distance. Yes, they were beautiful. Not something she'd see back home.

She noticed several more buildings on the grounds. A long, wooden building had saddles hooked over the railing that surrounded it. To the left was a barn with a corral. The smiling boy she saw earlier was brushing his horse there. The cowboy who'd been with him sat on the wooden fence, watching.

"Smell that air," Clint said. He took a deep breath.

She did. The scent of pine drifted on the air, but she'd rather smell coffee. "Which building is the dining room?"

He pointed. "Hang on a minute."

He gave a shrill whistle and waved to the cowboy and the boy. "Morning, Jake. Morning, Tyrone."

They waved back.

"That's Jake Dixon. I guess you could call him the program director of the Gold Buckle. Tyrone is a camper." He walked toward Susan, as if he had all the time in the world.

She groaned. "Coffee. Hurry."

But he didn't hurry. She waited for him and looked around. To her right, almost a city block away, stood a large ranch house that must have been the model for the dozen or so smaller cottages. From the beams of the wraparound porch, fuchsia-colored flowers cascaded from hanging baskets. Pink and red roses climbed on white trellises from a bountiful garden.

On one half of the porch was another set of stairs and a wheelchair ramp. A large sign on the roof proclaimed "Office."

There were still more buildings. Some were weathered, others were whitewashed, and some were stone or brick. It looked like a little village.

Clint arrived at her side, and she felt his hand at the small of her back.

"It's not like New York City, I suppose."

She had to admit it was a pretty setting. "Manhattan looks incredible at night, but here there's such wide-open space and all those trees and mountains. It's breathtaking."

"I never thought you'd notice."

"I didn't, until you pointed it out."

Clint laughed and offered his arm. "Shall we dine?"

She hesitated a moment, then took his arm. "Sure."

He motioned toward a chalet-type building with big picture windows. "That's the dining hall, movie hall and all-round gathering place. And there's always a pot of coffee on, day or night."

The man knew how to get to her—forget the Chardonnay, bring on the caffeine.

"I think I should call my office first and see how things are going."

"You've only been gone a day. Let's eat first."

"But I've never been gone a day before."

He shrugged. "Give them some space. Maybe it would show you trusted them."

Maybe he was right, but she was still going to call.

As they walked, Susan was very aware of his presence. She could feel his taut muscles beneath his shirt. The sound of his boots against the hard-packed ground reminded her of a hundred old western movies that her father used to watch on TV—when he was still around, anyway.

She studied Clint. He was clean-shaven, tanned and fit, and he was making her heart beat double time in her chest.

No one she'd ever dated had excited her this much. Admittedly, she'd always gone for typical Manhattan businessmen—stockbrokers, bankers, real estate developers—yet it was this cowboy who intrigued her the most.

Then again, she didn't really know Clint. Heaven knows that she had more in common with the Manhattan singles. She loved to talk business with them. But none of them were for her. None of them could handle it when she left them waiting at the restaurant or the latest trendy bar a couple of times because she had to stay late at work.

Clint opened the door for her and she walked in. One of the first things she noticed were the long rows of picnic tables lined up end to end. The dining hall was crowded and noisy with a lot of laughter, the clang of china plates and the metallic clicking of silverware.

And full of kids.

Susan's heart started to ache immediately. Yet these kids were smiling and laughing, yelling to one another. She could hear snippets of conversation about the horses they wanted to ride and what they planned to do during the day.

Black cowboy hats bobbed up and down, like a flock of crows pecking at seed. Every once in a while, a white hat could be spotted in the mix—a dove among the crows.

Under the hats were cowboys and cowgirls of all ages, wearing long-sleeved shirts, denim jeans and cowboy boots.

Uniforms. Cowboy uniforms.

She looked down at her designer clothes and her strappy Italian sandals. Maybe she ought to find a phone and give Bev a call, ask her to send a care package of western wear.

Clint steered her toward the back of the huge room to a cafeteria line, just like the one she remembered from high school. He plopped down an orange plastic tray in front of her and nodded to a tall, thin cowboy behind the counter. He had bristly white whiskers and a black baseball hat that read "Professional Bull Riders." He wore a gray T-shirt, and on his arms were tattoos of the Marine Corps.

"She wants the works, Cookie," Clint said.

Before she could tell him that she just wanted a toasted bagel with cream cheese, he handed her a plate heaped with scrambled eggs, bacon, ham and fried potatoes with onions.

"Come back for seconds or thirds if you want 'em," Cookie said, grinning. "We got more than enough."

Clint plucked a potato that had fallen off her plate onto the tray and popped it into his mouth. "Every once in a while, Cookie thinks that he's still cooking for the marines."

She looked down at her breakfast, floating in grease. "I see that he specializes in low-fat cuisine."

Cookie handed Clint an identically heaped plate of food.

"The grease makes your hair shiny," Clint said, leading Susan to an empty picnic table. "How do you take your coffee?"

"Black."

"Have a seat, I'll be right back."

She watched him walk to a round table supporting a coffee urn as big as a silo. Clint could really work a pair of jeans, and she could think of several designers who'd scoop him up instantly as a model, but her major concern was the fact that her coffee would be cold by the time he meandered back.

He finally returned and handed her a steaming mug of the coffee and she took a long sip. The strong, bitter brew slammed against the back of her brain and her eyes watered. She gasped for breath as her toes curled into her sandals.

"Good stuff, huh?" Clint said. "That's cowboy coffee."

She closed her eyes. She couldn't speak.

"You'll get used to it."

She took a bite of bacon. It had a nice smoky flavor and she guessed it was the real cholesterol-laden thing.

"So what are you going to teach in arts and crafts?" Clint asked. "I'll help you any way I can."

She took a deep breath. She didn't want to think about it yet. "Thanks, Clint. I appreciate the offer and will definitely take you up on it."

He nodded and concentrated on his plate of food.

"How come nobody takes their hat off when they eat?" Susan asked.

"A cowboy never takes his hat off," Clint replied. Then he winked. "Well, maybe there's one thing that I'd take my hat off for."

He winked again, and she felt a tingle in her belly. She might be rusty as to the flirting thing, but it was all coming back to her. "You're bald under that hat, right?"

"Like I said, I only take my hat off for one thing, so if you want to find out…"

There was that annoying flip of her heart again.

Before she could think of a witty comeback, she noticed a little girl on crutches awkwardly making her way toward the table. And all she could think of was Elaine, as a pang struck her heart.

How was she going to survive this trip when she couldn't escape her memories?

Chapter Four

Susan couldn't take her eyes off the little girl. She had blond wispy hair like Elaine's, and Elaine's smile, but that's where the similarity ended. Elaine had been much taller and weighed more than this tiny creature.

As the girl got closer, Susan could see that she had braces on both legs. A piece of paper and a pen were crumpled around the handle of a crutch where she clutched it.

She had a big grin as she made her way over to them. "Can I help you with something, sweetie?" Susan asked, trying to ignore her aching heart.

"I want Cheyenne Clint's autograph," she said.

Susan smiled at her. "Cheyenne who?"

The girl tilted her head. "Cheyenne Clint. The rodeo clown. He's sitting right next to you."

"Cheyenne Clint—" Susan laid her hand on his arm to get his attention "—you have a fan here who wants your autograph."

Clint wiped his mouth with a napkin and swiveled to see who was talking to him. "Well, well, aren't you a pretty young lady." He tipped his hat to her. "Cheyenne Clint Scully at your service, little lady."

The tiny girl giggled. "Will you sign your autograph?"

"I'd be honored." Clint patiently waited as she handed him the crumpled paper and a pen. "What's your name, darlin'?"

"Alisa Constance Pedigrew."

Clint gave a high-pitched whistle as he scribbled on the paper. "That's a name for a princess. Are you a princess?"

She giggled again, cocking her head to the side. "No." Her fine, pale hair skimmed the shoulder of her colorful striped T-shirt and then she tossed her head back. She had on a pair of denim shorts that hid the top of where her braces started. She leaned on aluminum crutches with metal armbands.

"Well, I am going to make you the Princess of

the Gold Buckle Ranch for as long as you stay here. That okay with you?"

"Sure!"

Clint made Alisa's face light up with pure enjoyment, and that was a real talent.

Clint took off his hat, and Susan saw that he had short, straight brown hair shot with streaks of gold. Mystery solved.

He placed his hat on Alisa's head and said, "I, Cheyenne Clint, pronounce you Princess of the Gold Buckle Ranch."

Alisa's giggle got louder and she leaned over to cover her mouth with a hand. She glanced around the room as if eager to see if anyone else might have noticed her coronation. Finally, she glanced at Susan, a certain shyness entering her gaze.

"Hello," she said. "Are you Mrs. Cheyenne Clint?"

Heaven forbid.

"No. My name is Susan. Susan Collins." Even to Susan's ears, her voice sounded thin and strained.

The little girl brushed back some of her hair from her face. The crutch dangled from her arm. "You're pretty."

"Why, thank you, Alisa. So are you." She didn't know what else to say. "Are you a camper?"

She nodded. "For a while. I'm an orphan, you know. I'm staying with Mrs. Dixon until I get adopted." A slightly defiant look entered her expressive blue eyes. "But Robbie says that because I'm six going on seven, and I'm handicapped, no one might want me. Do you think that's true?"

Susan swallowed hard, resisting the urge to scoop the girl up and hold her tight. Who the hell was Robbie and what made him say such a cruel thing? But Susan knew the answer to that. Kids could be cruel. They'd been cruel to Elaine. They used to grab her crutches and make her reach for them. No one ever asked her to play with them—it was as if she carried some contagious disease that they were afraid to catch. As her sister battled her bone cancer, all she'd ever wanted was to get better—so she could finally be invited to play with the other kids.

But how was she supposed to answer a question like that? To say, "Oh, that's not true" seemed so hollow. The girl was probably right. It was difficult to place older children for adoption, and those with medical problems were nearly impossible to find adoptive parents for.

She prayed that whatever was wrong with Alisa could be fixed with surgery, or maybe the braces would help mend her.

Clint reached out and gently tucked the little

girl's wispy blond hair behind her ear. "Tell me, who is this Robbie?"

"Oh, he's one of the boys in the foster home I was in, but he got adopted. He liked to tease everyone."

"I might have to have a little chat with Robbie. Can't have him teasing the Princess of the Gold Buckle Ranch, now, can we?"

Alisa and Clint exchanged grins, and she moved closer to him, her small body leaning up against his as if for protection.

"Thank you," she whispered.

"My pleasure. So Mrs. Dixon is taking care of you for a while, right?"

"Uh-huh. I was the only one left. The foster parents wanted to go on vacation, so my social worker asked Mrs. Dixon to let me stay here. And Mrs. Dixon said that I could ride the horses and be one of the Gold Buckle Gang. Cool, huh?"

"Cool. And I'll bet you'll be the best rider here."

Alisa looked much younger than "almost seven." She was too tiny for her age. Susan guessed that it might be due to her condition.

Her heart turned into a lead weight in her chest. It would be too easy to fall in love with this little girl.

Susan wouldn't—*couldn't*—let herself do that.

"Are you going to be working here?" Alisa asked.

"I'll be teaching arts and crafts."

Alisa's light blue eyes were sparkling now. "Are you going on the campout? Can I ride by you? Will you be my counselor?"

Susan tried to swallow so she could speak, but the words wouldn't come. Elaine, too, had looked at her with such hope and blind trust.

Susan had made Elaine promises that she couldn't keep. She'd said that she wouldn't let Elaine die, but she hadn't been able to keep that promise.

"I'm going to teach Susan how to ride," Clint said.

"Awesome." Alisa giggled, slipping Clint's autograph into the pocket of her shorts. "I gotta go now. I'm supposed to meet my social worker at Mr. and Mrs. Dixon's house."

Clint stood to his full height and bowed at the waist. "I'll see you later, Princess Alisa."

Susan watched as Alisa limped away. It seemed like such an effort for her little body to move, and Susan wanted to pick her up and carry her wherever she had to go.

But it was far better to keep her distance from the girl, and the other campers. Distance allowed her to keep the hurt and guilt from filling her up and choking her.

Distance and hard work. When she was working and busy, she forgot about Elaine and her parents. About how lonely she was.

Clint put his hand over hers and squeezed. "You look pretty shaken. Are you all right?"

"I'm fine." Susan knew her smile faltered a little, but she hid it behind her coffee cup.

"It's hard to see kids suffer like that."

More than you'll ever know.

"You were great with her." She liked the feel of his hand on hers.

Clint leaned in closer and grinned. "I'm even better with ladies your age."

She removed her hand. She didn't want him to think she was interested in a relationship with him, or anyone for that matter. "I didn't know what to say to her after she dropped the bomb about being an orphan." Susan took a sip of coffee, closed her eyes and waited for the bitter aftertaste to dissolve.

"You did fine," he said.

She'd wanted to assure Alisa that things would be okay, that she'd find two parents who would love her and they'd make a family. But Susan knew those kinds of wishes rarely came true. Growing up, Susan had prayed every evening for an intact family, but it hadn't happened. She'd asked Santa and wished upon all the stars in the sky, but still her father never came back to stay for good.

Remembering all those unanswered prayers

and dreams, she suddenly lost her appetite, but watched as Clint finished his breakfast. Then he washed it down with a long drag of coffee and didn't even blink.

"By the way, why are you called Cheyenne Clint?"

"Because I was born and raised in Boston."

She chuckled. "Okay, sorry. Dumb question, but you could be a Cheyenne Indian."

"Okay. I'm from Cheyenne, Wyoming. A while ago some announcer started calling me that, and it stuck. Now, are you ready to learn how to ride?" he asked.

She thought again of Alisa and the other kids. Although she wanted to help, she knew everyone would be better off if she just wrote out a check.

"Clint, I'm really not good with kids. Not like you are. Maybe you could teach arts and crafts."

Clint leaned back, his arms crossed. His eyes seemed to bore into her soul. The intensity of his gaze threw her and made her want to take back what she'd said. But the words hung in the air between them.

"What are you afraid of?" he finally said. "They're just kids. You'll do fine."

She almost believed him, but somewhere deep inside her a little voice told her he was wrong. He didn't know her history, her childhood. She wouldn't be fine. She knew this like she knew linen from cotton, jersey from wool. She was headed for a fall and powerless to steady herself.

But sink or swim, she'd live up to her promise.

Clint guided Susan through the open doors of the barn.

Even to her untrained eye, the interior was meticulously clean, in spite of the fact that a good three dozen horses, who had nothing to do except eat and poop, were in residence.

The gray cement floor was spotless, and the sweet smell of hay permeated the barn. Stalls flanked both sides of the aisle, and horses of various colors hung their heads over their half doors to inspect their visitors.

Clint looked at her sandals. "You should have changed your shoes for riding."

"I didn't bring any shoes for riding."

"What about running shoes?"

"I did bring a pair of those." Susan sighed. "I don't know about all this." She looked around the barn, then at Clint. "I don't belong here." So much about keeping her promises. So much for doing it for the kids. She was just one selfish woman.

Before she could stop him, Clint took her hand, slipped his arm around her waist and began to dance with her around the barn. He hummed a slow tune, something she didn't recognize, but oh, she liked it—and she liked being held by him.

"You're just nervous about riding. Relax a little."

She looked up into his eyes. He smiled and kept humming his tune. He was easy to dance with, easy to talk to. She didn't want to get to know him or confide in him. She just wanted out. That's all.

Instead, all her emotions were bubbling to the surface, things that she'd kept buried in her heart.

Susan knew exactly what had triggered it all: Alisa, the little girl she'd met at breakfast.

She wanted to push her emotions back down into that place where she'd kept them hidden all these years, but here, of all places, they just wouldn't stay put.

This must be how people with amnesia feel when their memory comes flooding back.

Clint must have sensed she was about to pull out of his arms, because he held her tighter and whispered, "Slow down, Susie. Just dance with me."

She swallowed the lump in her throat. "No one has called me that since my mother died."

"Tell me about her."

His soothing voice calmed her as his hand gently stroked circles on her back. As they spoke, he continued to slowly move her around the barn as if it were their own private dance hall.

"She died seven years ago. It was a heart attack. She died in her sleep."

Darn it. There was no holding her back now. She was really going to spill her guts to a cowboy she'd only met yesterday.

Susan took a deep breath. "My father left us periodically. He'd just pack up and head out for months at a time. He worked for a travel agency, and most of the times he was gone he'd be leading groups on tours. Later, he left more frequently and stayed away longer because he couldn't cope with…everything."

She'd managed to gather up enough sense to stop from telling him why her father couldn't cope. She wasn't ready to discuss Elaine.

"Mom was a nurse, so I never saw her much, either. She threw herself into her work to keep busy after Dad moved out for good."

"And then?"

"And then she started to do some sewing—alterations, tailoring, whatever she could do to make ends meet. Then she started making cute, colorful smocks for other nurses, and sold them. She showed me how to pin the patterns to the material. After I did my homework, I'd cut the material. Eventually we had quite a business going. I treasured the time with her. Later, during summer vacation from school, we'd make gowns for the patients. We'd make really fun ones for the kids with wild material and colors. As I got older, Mom taught me how to run the sewing machine."

She felt Clint's hand on her neck, under her hair, rubbing and kneading at the knot of tension. She let herself be boneless, loose.

"When my mother died, I started Winners Wear. It was a dream of ours."

"And you made your company a success."

It was a statement, not a question, and she liked that.

"I have," she said proudly.

"Good for you. And your father?"

"What about him?"

"Did he ever come back into the picture?"

"No." Susan felt the usual apathy and bitterness well up inside her whenever she thought of her father. "Apparently he has a pretty successful travel agency of his own now."

He left right after Elaine died—hadn't even come to the funeral. He was taking a tour group to Greece. Susan had only been twelve years old, and she'd needed her father. Her mother had been inconsolable, wrapped up in her own sadness.

She'd never forgiven her father for deserting them.

What was she doing spilling her guts to a bull-fighter? She'd seen some of the best counselors in

New York, and had never blabbed like she did to this man in a barn full of horses.

After a while, it seemed like the most natural thing in the world to dance in a barn and tell a stranger about her life. It was okay, she told herself. She'd never see him again after this week.

She closed her eyes and listened to Clint hum. His chest vibrated with each note, each nuance of the tune. She tried to relax her mind and not think about orders for football jerseys or the Idaho marching band with the potato on their lapels. She tried not to think about her father, or how she missed her mother and Elaine. Or how much Alisa reminded her of Elaine.

She simply closed her eyes and concentrated on dancing with this unique cowboy.

The dancing stopped and Clint still held her in his arms. He studied her face, then drew closer. His eyes lowered as if he were studying her lips.

She could hear his breathing increase as he tipped his head.

She wouldn't object if he kissed her. She wanted him to kiss her. Maybe then she'd stop wondering what it would be like.

Instead, he gave a slight wink, tweaked his hat and let her go.

Chapter Five

He'd almost kissed her.

Normally, he would have, but for whatever reason, he had held himself back. But why? He could tell that Susan was willing.

There had to be something seriously wrong with Clint Scully if he'd stopped himself from kissing a beautiful woman.

Who was he kidding? He knew the reason. Mary Alice Bonner still haunted him. She'd had the same expensive tastes and the same drive for success as Susan, the same determination to prove that they could succeed.

Susan had proved that she didn't need her father.

Mary Alice had proved that she didn't need Clint Scully.

While he'd been waiting for the wedding march to begin at St. Paul's Church in Cheyenne, Mary Alice had been on a plane to Chicago.

She had sent him a note via her sister, Louise, so at least he hadn't waited all day for her, wondering what had happened. The note had read simply, "Sorry, Clint. I want something more than you can give me."

More than you can give me.

Mary Alice Bonner was now the president of a Fortune 500 jewelry chain, a member of the jet set and a regular in *People* magazine.

He frequently ran into Mary Alice's sister, Louise. Lou said that Mary Alice wasn't all that happy, and had paid a high price for her success.

Susan Collins was all New York City, from the top of her sleek coppery-red hair down to her pedicured toes with the pink polish. She was a successful businesswoman from what he could tell, too. She was smart, had a bossy side, and yet something still gnawed at her.

He could also tell that when she wasn't comfortable in a situation, she wanted to retreat. She still might bolt yet.

Just like Mary Alice Bonner.

Susan was intriguing—and Clint really liked

intriguing—but he couldn't get involved with her. No way in hell. He might have taken a few blows in the head from some bulls, but he wasn't stupid.

"Pick out a horse you like," he said. "All of them are as gentle as lambs and have been trained for the Wheelchair Rodeo kids."

"Therefore, we city slickers can handle them, too?"

"Absolutely."

"Okay."

"I'll have you riding before you can say, 'Big Apple,' so don't worry about a thing." He put a hand on her back and could feel the tension in the set of her spine, tension that had almost dissolved when they were dancing.

She continued walking, then stopped to pet the nose of a pretty palomino. "I like this one. She's smiling at me."

Clint rubbed a hand along his chin. "Yep, she's definitely smiling at you."

"What's her name?"

He pointed to the sign above the stall. "Goldie."

She ran her hand along the horse's neck. "Hello, Goldie."

"Watch how I saddle her up, and from now on you can do it." Clint lifted a bridle from the nail next to Goldie's stall and saw Susan checking her watch.

He tightened the girth on the saddle. "Did you get all that? How I saddled and bridled the horse?"

"Absolutely," she said, shaking her head no.

"Great." He chuckled and handed her the reins. "Goldie will be your horse for as long as you're here. You'll both have to get used to each other. Walk her out to the corral."

She tightened her hands around the reins. "Okay, Goldie. Let's go."

Susan was gentle with Goldie and frequently looked back to see if the horse was still attached to the reins and still following her. A lot of first-time riders did the same thing, and he always got a kick out of it.

He walked beside her out to the corral. "Okay. Now take the reins and put them on each side of her neck and keep them in your hand." He held the bridle. "Okay. Good. Put your left foot in the stirrup and toss your right leg over the saddle."

"Um…uh…she's pretty high up there."

"Yup."

"No steps?" At least there had been steps where she took lessons.

"No. And she won't squat down for you like a camel, either."

"You read my mind."

She put her foot in the stirrup and did three

hops. On her next hop, Clint grabbed her cute bottom and gave her an extra boost into the saddle.

"Was it good for you?" he asked.

She chuckled and rolled her eyes, then concentrated on the horse. "I never realized that they were this tall."

He wished he had a dollar for every time he heard that, he thought, slipping a hand under a bridle strap. "I'll just walk her around the corral for a while so you can get used to her. Just relax and feel the rhythm of her gait. Go with it."

He walked the horse for ten minutes, stealing glances at Susan. She looked like a queen on her throne, smiling, glancing around and petting the horse's neck.

Clint stopped. "Are you ready to do this yourself?"

"Sure."

He let go of the bridle and held his hands up as if he were being arrested. "Go nice and slow. Nothing fancy. Just walk her around the corral. Big circle. She knows what do."

He hopped up on the fence, leaned his elbows on his thighs and flagged down a cowboy walking by. "Juan, do you have time to saddle up Brutus for me? I don't want to leave our guest alone here. She's a genuine city slicker."

"Will do, Clint."

"Thanks, *amigo*."

Clint watched as Susan rode Goldie at a slow walk around the corral. It was a beautiful scene with the blue skies, a beautiful horse and a beautiful woman, not necessarily in that order. However, the beautiful woman was about to jar her brains loose.

"Keep your heels down, Susan," he shouted. "Go with the rhythm of the horse."

She did as instructed and the results were much smoother.

He let her do that for another five minutes until she yelled, "Hey, we're getting dizzy here."

"Just lean the reins lightly on her neck, lead her over here and hit the brakes."

"Brakes?"

"Just kidding. She'll stop on her own."

"I knew that," she said.

Juan brought Brutus over, and Clint hopped down from the fence. "Thanks."

Juan couldn't take his eyes off of Susan. Clint slapped him on the back and lightly pushed him along his way. "Thanks again, *amigo*. Bye, now."

Finally, Juan took the hint.

"How about a ride on the Chisholm Trail?" Clint asked.

"I'm not familiar with this part of the world, but isn't that a little far away?"

"We have what we call the Chisholm Trail right

here. It runs behind the cabins and alongside the creek. Shall we?"

He nudged Brutus along. Goldie would follow Brutus, so Susan didn't have much choice but to follow him.

No matter how intriguing her secrets were, he couldn't help but wish that he were on the real Chisholm Trail, far away from her.

He knew danger. He dealt with it every time the chute gate opened and a bull came charging out with a cowboy on his back.

Susan was a different kind of danger. She was everything he wasn't.

She was asphalt and high rises. He was prairie grass and mountains. She was designer clothes and Italian sandals. He was jeans and boots.

Still, she was the kind of woman that made a cowboy think about hanging up his spurs and settling down.

Not that he was that kind of cowboy.

No one would ever get him to settle down and work himself to death. His parents had done that. Susan was doing that.

He liked being free.

Susan wasn't the type who'd ever like the road. She'd never even seen a bull riding event. At least Mary Alice had traveled with him for a while.

He didn't even know why he was even thinking along those lines about Susan Collins. He never usually thought about making a life with the women who crossed his path, let alone anything beyond one night.

In spite of all their differences, it didn't mean that they couldn't enjoy each other for a week. When it was over, he'd just say goodbye.

The way he always did.

Goldie dutifully followed Brutus down the so-called Chisholm Trail, and Susan just sat as if she were in a rocking chair. She kept her heels down as Clint had instructed, and checked her watch to see what time it was back home.

"Clint, can we get back? I really need to make some calls."

"Will you relax and quit worrying about what's happening at your company." He glanced over one broad shoulder, a small smile touching the corners of those magnificent lips—lips that hadn't kissed her in the barn for whatever reason. "Look around you. It's beautiful out here."

Gripping the saddle horn, she did look around, realizing with a certain amount of wonder that he was right. The rays of the sun lit up the pine trees and released their scent. On their right side, a little brook sparkled, its slow-running current meandering over rocks and dips and making cheerful, soothing noises.

She noticed the sun hovering over the peaks and bathing the valley in sunlight—sunlight that filtered through the pines.

She let herself smell the pine-scented air and feel the slight breeze on her face. She listened to the water and the steady clip-clop of the horses. For a while, she was so relaxed that she was afraid she'd fall asleep and fall out of the saddle.

There was no denying the fact that time moved slower at the Gold Buckle. As slow as the laid-back cowboy riding in front of her.

Who would have thought that she'd ever be riding through the woods of Wyoming with a cowboy?

The trail widened, and he slowed down to ride beside her. "Look at those little purple wildflowers up there."

She saw a cascade of purple on an embankment. Above the flowers, in a small clearing, stood a big white trailer.

"Who lives there?" Susan asked.

His horse stopped, and so did hers.

"That is Casa de Clint Scully. My house. I tow it wherever I go. Rodeo to rodeo…wherever."

"You live in *that?*"

His eyes twinkled. "It's a home on wheels. Want to see the inside? She's a beauty."

She nodded. "I see." But she didn't. Why would anyone want to live in such a thing? "Is there a washer and dryer in it?"

"No room. Matter of fact, if I gain five pounds, I can't turn around in it."

"Then who does your laundry? Your shirts are always impeccable and the crease down the arm is perfect."

"This is the way they come out of the package." He pointed to the logo on the front pocket. "My sponsors send them to me by the case."

"You have sponsors?"

"Several. I wear their stuff, and they get free advertising, especially when I'm on TV."

"You're on TV? Really?"

"Some bull riding events are televised. I told you before that Cheyenne Clint is a bona fide star."

He went up a notch in her estimation. Maybe he actually made a living out of his strange profession. Then she looked skeptically at his trailer.

He grinned, obviously knowing what she was thinking. "C'mon. I'll show you inside."

Goldie followed Brutus up a slight incline. Clint expertly got off Brutus and flipped the reins over a tree branch. He took Goldie's reins from her and did the same.

She started to get down from the horse but felt his hands on her waist, helping her down. She turned toward him, but his hands didn't move. Her body heated where he touched her.

She looked toward the trailer, and he cleared his throat.

"Uh…over here." He pointed.

They walked to a screen door on the other side of the trailer. He hit a button and three steps slid out. "Welcome."

Clint flicked on a switch and she could see that the inside was heaped from floor to ceiling with boxes.

"Your wardrobe?" she asked.

"All free of charge."

She was amazed at the oak cabinets, the granite counter, the microwave and the four-burner stove. A full-size refrigerator with a water and ice dispenser stood next to a dinette with seating for four. A beige leather couch was on the opposite side and a plasma TV and music equipment were positioned in a corner cabinet. All the cabinets were oak, the colors beige and light.

"Clint, this is just beautiful."

"You have to see the bathroom," he said, grabbing her hand and pulling her along.

His bathroom was bigger than the one in her apartment. So was the shower.

"Where's your bedroom?"

"Right here. And watch this."

He pressed a button, and the room slid out several feet. It gave the room much more space. There was a full-size queen bed and closets all around the room, another TV, nightstands and a vanity where he had a laptop and printer.

"This is incredible. It's designed so perfectly. Not an inch of space is wasted."

Later, they sat under the awning outside, sipping some ice water and listening to the water cascade over the rocks. Clint walked the horses to the creek and let them drink.

They spent an enjoyable hour just talking. Susan couldn't believe she just sat for such a long time doing nothing. She noticed everything about Clint—his easy manner of talking, the way he leaned forward and listened intently whenever she was speaking.

She couldn't remember when she had a better time.

"We should probably get going," Clint said.

He helped her back onto Goldie, pushing her butt with an exaggerated grunt.

She laughed. "Oh, stop."

"So, is trailer life for you?" he asked when they were back on the Chisholm Trail.

"I don't think so."

"What would you like?"

She thought about that for a while. She'd liked

when her family lived in Tarrytown, New York, when she was growing up in a Dutch colonial with a lot of nooks and crannies inside and a front and backyard. It was a great place to live and to go to school. She'd had friends there, friends who had since all gone their separate ways, but who still got together twice a year for dinner. They always asked her to go, but she was always too busy.

Funny, she hadn't thought about Tarrytown in a long time. She'd been happy there, at least for a while.

"If I ever decided to move out of Manhattan, which I never would, I might like a home with some land and a thick green lawn that needs mowing twice a week. And a garden where I can grow flowers and tomatoes."

"Sounds like a prison to me," he said.

"I suppose it does to someone who has a trailer and no roots."

He chuckled. "Just like a tumbling tumbleweed."

"Just like my father," she said. "Only he had a family that he ignored."

He frowned. "I don't have that problem."

That was true, so he could do what he wanted. So could she.

They walked out of the woods into the meadow

that lay like a carpet of wildflowers up to the base of the mountain. She had the urge to see how fast Goldie could go.

"Could we gallop, Clint?"

"No. You're too new at this. But how about a trot? Keep your legs down. Don't bounce."

Brutus went faster, and Goldie followed. Clint picked up more speed.

She laughed. She was a kid again at her Saturday riding lesson. She could picture her father cheering for her. Later, they'd take the train back to Tarrytown.

They'd stop for a cheeseburger and chocolate shake at Casey's Corner. All too soon, the weekend would be over. Monday was school again, and her responsibilities would return. She always had to watch over Elaine in school, protect her from the other kids.

What would it be like to have no responsibility like Clint?

She couldn't fathom it. She had more than four hundred people who depended on her for their income.

Clint slowed down and they went back to a walk. He pulled his horse up next to hers. Clint was born to sit in a saddle. His jean-clad thighs looked rock hard, and he seemed natural and relaxed, as if he could ride all day. Yet underneath that exterior, he was a little wild and untamed, and Susan couldn't picture him living anywhere except under the Western skies.

She was breathing hard and could barely talk. "Before I leave, I'd like to gallop."

"You're a tough woman, Susan Collins."

"You ain't seen nothing yet, Cheyenne Clint."

Chapter Six

Emily Dixon rushed into the barn while they were brushing their horses.

"You're just the two I've been looking for. Susan, I have to cancel our meeting about the arts and crafts program until later this afternoon. I'm sorry."

"That's okay, Emily," Susan said, although she was disappointed at the news. She wanted to brainstorm some projects.

Emily flipped through her clipboard. "Clint, I noticed that you aren't scheduled for any activities until this afternoon."

"What's up, Mrs. D?" Clint asked.

"Alisa's group is scheduled for a riding lesson, but I can't let her participate. She's inconsolable. It's a paperwork and insurance problem with Children's Services. She has to be cleared by their doctor, and he's not available. Right now, she's crying on her bed up at the house. She's asking for you both."

"Me?" Susan asked. "I barely know her."

"She has connected with you somehow." Emily smiled.

Clint grinned. "Of course."

"I don't know what to do. All I can think of is that maybe she'd like a picnic and a splash in the river. I don't mean to impose, but I have a lot of things to do and—"

"You were wondering if we could help?" Clint said.

"Please?" Emily asked.

Clint nodded. "I'm in the mood for a picnic and a splash in the river. How about you, Susan?"

She'd rather not. It was obvious that Alisa was already getting too attached to them both, but her heart went out to the girl. She had been excluded, like Susan's own sister had always been, so if a picnic and a swim would make her feel as though she belonged, then Susan would go.

She nodded. "Sounds like fun."

"Let's do it, then." He cracked his knuckles. "Mrs. D, tell Alisa to dry her eyes, slip her bathing suit on and wait for us in front of the office. Susan, you do the same."

Emily let out a deep breath. "I'll get Cookie to pack up a nice lunch." She smiled gratefully. "I can't thank you both enough."

A half hour later, Clint was lifting Alisa into the buckboard. Then he helped Susan in. They jostled and swayed, singing songs at the top of their lungs, until they finally arrived at the picnic area.

Clint pointed to a clapboard building. "That's a combination changing area, shower facility and bathroom. Some cowboys and I built it a couple years ago."

The building had a dusting of old rust-colored pine needles on the roof. It smelled like fresh-cut lumber, and looked sturdy enough to withstand whatever Wyoming weather it needed to. Then she noticed a sign: The Gold Buckle Ranch Thanks Clint Scully.

Susan turned to him. "You donated this…building?"

He nodded. "I told them not to put up that sign, but Mrs. D insisted."

She smiled. "That was very generous of you." It must have cost him everything he had.

"It was nothing. I'm only regretting that we didn't make it bigger, so I figure I'll have to donate another one."

Susan wondered whether he was joking.

She turned to see a wide concrete path that led to a glittering river. Green picnic tables were scattered along the bank.

Susan took a deep breath. "It's a beautiful day for a picnic."

Clint raised an eyebrow. "You noticed?"

"Yes. I've noticed."

He jumped down from the buckboard and tied the horses to a post. "Maybe there's hope for you yet."

He came around to her side, offered her his hand and helped her down.

"Thanks."

"My pleasure."

It *was* surprising that she was noticing anything lately. Clint was occupying her thoughts much too much. He made her laugh like she hadn't in years, and she was relaxed around him. Maybe too relaxed. A part of her regretted telling him such personal things about her life. She'd always taken great pride in being able to keep things about her family safely stored and locked tightly inside her. Here, she had way too much free time to think, to unlock her feelings and look inside.

She needed to keep busy. Needed to concentrate on concrete things, like shipping, filling orders, the payroll, the IRS. Those were tangible things that occupied her days and nights in calm, rational ways. She didn't need these emotional feelings that pulled and tore at her very being. That's why she needed to get back to New York.

Alisa appeared at her side. "Susan, could you tie my bathing suit for me? It came undone."

"Sure, sweetie."

Alisa bent her head, and Susan quickly tied her little halter top in place.

"Great suit," Susan said, trying not to notice the way Alisa's right hip protruded from her skinny body. Her right knee looked a little swollen and pinkish near one of the bars of her brace, but Susan knew that this was common. Elaine had suffered from her braces on numerous occasions. The cold river water would help that.

"Look! There's a bird's nest in that tree," Alisa shouted.

Susan looked up, following the line of Alisa's finger. "I see it. It's a pretty big one."

"Can we look closer at it?"

"Sure."

Just as they were walking over to the tree, Clint appeared at their side.

"What's up?" he asked.

"There's a bird's nest in that tree. I want to see if there are any babies in it," Alisa said.

Clint put a finger up to his lips. "We have to

quietly make sure there *aren't* any babies in it, or it'll bother the mother bird."

They crept closer to the nest and leaned over.

"I don't see any babies," Alisa whispered.

"I don't, either," Clint agreed. "I think everyone's moved out."

Susan could feel his breath on her neck and could smell his spicy aftershave. If she turned slightly, she'd be mouth-to-mouth with him.

The thought sent a delicious shiver through her.

"Can I have it?" Alisa asked.

Susan turned to look around for a feathered home owner who might object, and her eyes met Clint's. She could get lost in those turquoise eyes of his, the color of the Wyoming sky overhead.

"I can't ever say no to a beautiful lady," Clint said, gazing into Susan's eyes.

He sure could flirt, and she was rusty, but she leaned over and whispered in his ear, "Can you reach it?"

She could hear his quick intake of air. He turned toward her, and their lips almost touched. She didn't move. He blinked and swallowed hard.

"Um…uh…" His voice sounded rough, wheezy. "I'll get the nest for you, Alisa."

"Thanks."

She watched as Clint placed the nest so very gently into Alisa's hands. Tears welled up in

Susan's eyes as she watched him. It was a little thing, but something shot straight to her heart. Could he be any sweeter?

They waited as Alisa examined every inch of the nest. The look of complete awe on her face made Susan smile.

Had she ever been that young, that happy? When had she ever stepped off her treadmill to notice a bird's nest in a pine tree?

"Could I have a pinecone, too?" Alisa lifted up a crutch and pointed to a top branch. "Could I have that one, please?"

"Of course, sweetie." Susan plucked it off and handed it to her.

The girl inspected it carefully just as she inspected the bird's nest.

"Don't you guys want pinecones?"

Clint nodded. "Absolutely."

"Sure," Susan said, wondering what on earth she'd do with a pinecone.

Susan plucked two more from the tree and handed them to Alisa.

"Awesome."

"Let's put them here for now." Susan pointed to the nest, and Alisa dropped them in. "And we'll put the nest on top of the tote bag."

Clint clapped his hands together and rubbed them. "Let's head for the water."

"Don't forget the picnic supplies back at the wagon," Susan reminded him.

"Well, just call me a pack mule," he said, loping off to the wagon.

"Cheyenne Clint is funny." Alisa looked up at her, her head tilted and her eyes squinted into the sun. "Do you like him?"

"Sure. He's funny and happy all the time. Right?"

Alisa nodded. "My dad was funny, too. Me and my mom were always laughing at him." She looked at the water, and then looked down. "Will you help me take the braces off?"

Elaine used to say that to her. Used to look up at her that way. *"Please, Susie, help me take this stuff off."*

"Of course I'll help you."

"I'll show you how."

"I know how, Alisa. I know."

"You do?"

"My sister Elaine had to wear braces."

"Really?"

Susan nodded.

"Does she still have to wear them? Or did she get better?"

"She didn't get better." Susan took a deep breath, and felt the usual sting in the back of her eyes whenever she thought of Elaine. She looked away so that Alisa wouldn't see the water in them. "Elaine is…uh…no longer with us."

Alisa's eyes grew wide. "Elaine went to heaven?"

Susan nodded, not trusting herself to talk.

Susan felt Alisa's little fingers wiggling their way into her hand. She looked down at the sweet, small face of the little girl who was slowly but surely sneaking into her heart.

"My mommy and daddy are in heaven, too," Alisa said.

Susan closed her eyes. She couldn't allow herself to love another girl who looked at her as if she could rope the moon.

Another little girl she might lose.

Susan didn't want to know if Alisa's condition was terminal. Some things were better left unsaid or unknown, or the pain would be unbearable.

Susan glanced over at Clint, who was still back at the wagon, unloading all the things that Emily had sent. She wished he were here to say or do something funny and ease this sudden sad moment.

Well, he wasn't, so it was up to her.

She mustered a smile, gave Alisa's hand a squeeze and knelt on the grass in front of her. "Let's get rid of all that metal and plastic, shall we?"

She unhooked Alisa's braces, slipped them off, and then removed the girl's shoes and socks.

Looking like the pack mule he had joked about, Clint arrived. He carried a picnic basket, a brightly striped blanket, two big gym bags and another tote bag.

He paused when he saw what Susan had done. She nodded slightly, so he'd get the message that things were okay.

He shook out the blanket and spread it on the grass. Opening a gym bag, he peered in and pulled out a small camp chair and a clip-on sun umbrella.

"Emily packed this for Alisa."

"Perfect," Susan said, taking the chair from him and unfolding it. They could put it in the water for Alisa to sit on. If she got sleepy, she could lie on the blanket under the shade of the umbrella. "She thought of everything."

They watched as Alisa wobbled unsteadily to the shore of the river with her bare feet and crutches.

Clint sat on the blanket and yanked off his boots and slid off his socks. "Hang on there, Miss Alisa. Don't put another toe in the water until we're with you."

"Hurry up, then," she ordered.

Clint unbuttoned his shirt, tossed it on the blanket and hurried to Alisa. Seeing his tanned, muscular chest gave Susan an immediate vision of him taking his shirt off for her as they made love.

She swallowed the lump in her throat, waiting

until her heart was beating normally again. Then she kicked off her sandals and slipped out of her clothes, picked up the chair and joined them. She walked out into the cold, clear water, which was only about seven inches deep, but ripe with rocks and stones. She immediately regretted not leaving a T-shirt on over her bathing suit for warmth.

"Yeow! This is cold," Susan said, ready to retreat.

"C'mon, chicken," Alisa yelled, splashing Susan.

Susan turned away from the freezing water only to catch Clint ready to splash her, too. "Don't you dare, Clint Scully. Let me get used to this…melting glacier."

"How about if we put this chair in the water and you can sit and splash as much as you want?" Clint said to Alisa.

"Okay."

Clint took the crutches from her and set them on the grass. They both took one of Alisa's hands, and waded slowly back into the river.

Clint unfolded Alisa's chair. "Your throne, Princess."

"Thank you, Cheyenne Clint."

Alisa sat down and immediately kicked up her feet, sending out glittering droplets of water. She giggled and started singing a song that Susan recognized from the movie *Cinderella*.

Susan waded out farther even though her feet

were numb with cold. She couldn't believe how clear the water looked, how lazily it gurgled. At her feet was an outcropping of semisubmerged rocks where the water pooled and swirled.

Clint must have been following her gaze. He gave her a nudge with his shoulder, and pointed. "There's a whirlpool."

"I'm tempted to sit right in it."

"So what's stopping you?"

Sinking into the natural whirlpool was a once-in-a-lifetime thing.

Alisa was singing and splashing not even four feet from them, and seemed to forget that they were nearby.

"She's having a ball," Clint said.

Susan lowered herself slowly into the froth of water. Gasping, she didn't realize how cold it would be.

"You won't notice the cold after a while." Clint stretched out next to her. "Great, isn't it?"

"Mmm…heavenly." She lifted her face to the sun, took a deep breath of fresh air and smiled at the handsome cowboy sitting beside her.

She couldn't stop her eyes from straying to his chest, so she gave up trying.

Clint was buff. She knew that from their dance in the barn, but she never realized how buff. She wanted to see even more of him.

"Oh," she said, noticing a U-shaped scar that traveled from his tight pecs to his even tighter abdomen. "Clint, did a bull give you that big scar?"

"Yup. A two-thousand-pound Brahman with a four-foot rack got me at the Billings event last year. I had a protective vest on, but he hooked me under it. Lost a couple buckets of blood, got a couple hundred stitches and spent a couple of days in the hospital. No problem."

She could just imagine the pain he'd suffered. "For heaven's sake, Clint. You could have died."

"Nah."

She moved toward him slowly, her index finger outstretched, suddenly wanting to touch the toughened skin of his scar. She stopped when she saw the sparkle in his eyes. "May I?"

"Be my guest." His voice seemed lower, huskier.

She ran her finger from the muscles of his arm to his abdomen where it disappeared into the waistband of his jeans. Her hand lingered there, then she traced the scar back up.

If she wasn't mistaken, Clint was holding his breath.

She followed the path of another scar. This one looked pinker, newer.

"Phoenix, Arizona." His voice had gotten softer and she could see a vein pumping in his temple.

Could it be that just her light touch bothered him? She liked that idea, so she traced the scar back up his arm.

"Did it hurt?"

"Not like the horn I took in Vegas." His hands clasped his zipper, and her mouth suddenly became dry.

He glanced over at Alisa, then his glittering eyes settled on Susan. He chuckled. "Sorry, you'll have to wait for another time to see that one."

She swallowed hard—the temperature had just gone up a few hundred degrees.

His gaze settled on her breasts, and his smile faded. When she looked down, she saw that her nipples were way too perky in the cold water. With her index finger and thumb, she plucked the fabric away from her body, but it didn't help much.

"You are *so* high school," she said, heart pounding.

His eyes twinkled. "You are *so* right."

"Let's get back to your job," she said. "All those scars, Clint. Why do you do it if it's so risky?"

"It's fun and it pays great for about three hours of work on a Saturday night. I can contract for as many or as few events as I want."

"I take it you don't like to work."

"Not when I don't have to."

"I live to work," she said proudly, trying not

to notice the beads of water glittering on his tanned skin.

"And I work to live. There's a big difference. My living expenses are nothing much. My sponsors keep me in clothes. I tow my trailer around with my used truck. During the summer, I'm here."

Strange way to live. "But you don't have any roots or benefits or a pension plan. Your medical insurance alone must cost a fortune."

"Roots are overrated, and no legitimate insurance company will insure me for less than a fortune, but I need insurance so I pay for it. As for a pension, I give a good chunk of my money to a bullfighter pal who invests it for me. That should take care of my old age, which is about age thirty in my business, and I'm already pushing that."

"A bullfighter pal invests for you? You must make a fortune." She didn't try to keep the sarcasm from her voice. "At least let me give you the name of someone reliable, someone on Wall Street."

"No way." He shook his head. "I'm doing okay with Cletus the Clown."

"Cletus the Clown. You've lost your mind. Nothing like throwing your money away."

He shrugged. "Clete's done a good job."

Since he didn't care about a place to live or

getting a real job, she didn't know why it surprised her that he didn't care about an important thing like investing wisely.

She thought about his lackadaisical attitude as she watched two little rivulets of water trickle down his chest, down his flat stomach, and disappear into his waistband.

She ran her wet hands over her face to cool off. It didn't help when she saw him watching her, smiling…knowing.

She turned and smiled at Alisa, who was still kicking up buckets of water. Alisa grinned back without missing a note of her latest song about fish under the sea.

"Tell me, Clint, what scares you about working?"

"I work hard at what I do."

"You know what I mean. A real job. Don't all cowboys have a ranch?"

His smile faded and he seemed a million miles away.

"I do have a ranch—a very profitable ranch. It sits on more than a thousand acres a couple hundred miles from here. I call it the Lazy S, for Scully. It fits, don't you think?"

A very profitable ranch.

"You're not lazy at all, Clint. You've accomplished a lot. And from what you've just told me, you're a rich man."

He took off his hat and stared inside the bowl of it as if it contained a crystal ball. "Money isn't everything. Everyone knows that. It doesn't buy…"

"Health? Real friends? Someone who loves you for who you are? A family to live in your house at the Lazy S?"

He raised an eyebrow at Susan after her last sentence. His half smile was particularly wistful, and she could see the loneliness in his eyes. She wanted to take his hand and hold it, to somehow connect with him and to let him know that she could identify with him.

Because she was lonely, too.

"Yes," he answered. "I'd love my parents back there, my sister and brother and their spouses and all their kids, along with my wife and kids. Everyone— back on the ranch. That'd be a dream come true."

Susan blinked back the tears that threatened to fall. Except for her estranged father, she didn't have a family anymore.

"It'll never happen," he said. "They have their own lives."

She could see how hard it was for him to talk about his family. "You never know," she said, trying to be upbeat.

"I do know." His jaw hardened, and his tone was bitter. "Happiness doesn't come cheap, and my family already paid the price."

Chapter Seven

Susan looked at Clint with a mixture of pity and shock.

He didn't want her pity, but she did deserve an explanation. She'd been nothing but kind, and he thought he could see the glistening of tears in her eyes.

That touched him.

Clint looked down at the water, remembering the river that ran alongside the Lazy S. It flowed deeper and faster when the snow melted. About now, he could probably jump it.

"Let me explain," he said. "My parents worked from sunrise to sunset to keep their ranch going.

We ran about three hundred head of cattle, a few dozen quarter horses and a couple dozen bulls. My sister and brother and I helped them before school, after school and every damn weekend, but we were fighting a losing battle."

He paused, lost in thought, remembering how he'd wanted nothing more than to rope, drink beer and travel to rodeos with Joe Watley and Jake Dixon, but gave it all up to return home to help his folks.

"They let the hands go to save money. They'd sold off stock, some land, but it just wasn't enough. My parents tried. We all tried. In the end, we all watched the auction sign being nailed up on the barn and the house."

"I can imagine how they felt," Susan said. "I'd hate it if I lost Winners Wear. I came close a couple of times, but then, like a miracle, a big order or two would come in and I could keep it going."

"My folks never got a miracle." He took her hand and stared at it. "I watched the light go out in their eyes. Then I swore I'd never let that happen to me. I was going to enjoy my life. See the world. Not care about a chunk of dirt."

"Are your parents still alive?"

"Alive and well in a seniors condo in Fort Myers, Florida. They play in pitch tournaments and take bus trips to the theme parks and the casinos. I bought them a huge motor home that they travel in when they want to visit my sister and her kids in St. Louis or my brother and his kids in New Orleans. Once in a while, they'll show up at a bull riding event and spend some time with me."

"You bought them a motor home?"

He nodded.

"I'll bet you bought them their condo, too."

He grinned.

"Good for you, Clint. Then it's a happy ending?"

"Yeah. They got off the treadmill they were on. Actually, they didn't have a choice, since the place was sold out from under them."

"Treadmill," she mumbled. She removed her hand from his and rubbed her forehead. She'd used that word earlier to describe her own hectic life. "I'm happy that things worked out for them."

"Me, too."

"Now, tell me more about your ranch," she said.

"I bought my parents' ranch from the latest owner and offered it back to them." He sat up a little taller, and Susan could tell that he was proud of that fact. "But they didn't want it anymore. They were enjoying their retirement."

Susan couldn't believe all that he'd accomplished. "You bought the family ranch back?"

"I did."

"Why aren't you there?"

"Because I'm here, helping out with the summer programs. My uncle Charlie is running things for me, and doing a great job."

Susan was astonished. "And you have sponsors. You also get paid for bullfighting, and—"

"And I'm partners with my friend Joe Watley in some ventures."

"You really have a big empire, cowboy."

He shrugged, never comfortable talking about money. "I do all right."

"Would you mind giving me Cletus the Clown's phone number?"

He laughed. "So, I went up a couple rungs on your ladder of rodeo bums?"

"Amazing." She shook her head. "Amazing… and now I think that we ought to get our singing mermaid to dry land," Susan said.

Clint stood and helped Susan to her feet. "What do you say, Alisa? Time for lunch?"

"Aw…"

"Come on. Picnic time," Clint said.

The three of them walked hand in hand back to the grassy bank.

Clint looked at Alisa sleeping on the blanket. Susan had set up the umbrella to keep the girl in the shade.

Susan looked like she was dozing off next to

Alisa, too. Never did he expect that the hyper New York could calm down enough to actually sleep.

The picnic lunch was a hit with ham and cheese sandwiches, lemonade and chunks of watermelon. Mrs. D had even included a deck of Old Maid playing cards that he was currently winging into the bowl of his upturned hat so he wouldn't keep staring at the front of Susan's shirt.

She'd rolled up a jacket and placed it under her neck as she lay on her back. The perfect mounds of her breasts rose and lowered with each inhale and exhale of breath. The fabric of her tank top had molded itself to her damp bathing suit.

He got up from the bench of the picnic table, collected the cards and straightened them into a tight deck. He scanned the area, making sure there weren't any two-legged, four-legged or no-legged creatures in the area that aimed to harm the two lovely ladies on the blanket.

Sitting back on the bench, he resumed tossing the cards. He loved being outdoors, no matter what weather, and liked these quiet times where he could just pass the day thinking…or not.

He was becoming quite fond of Susan and Alisa. Susan, for the obvious reason that she was damn sexy, easy to talk to and fun to be with most of the time. Alisa because she was the sweetest little girl he'd ever laid eyes on. He admired them both, each struggling with things in her own way, both fiercely independent—and both lonely.

He might as well add himself to that mix. Susan didn't have close family ties, and Alisa had lost her parents in a car accident. As for him, he had a lot of good friends, several of them female, but most all of his good buddies were busy with their own lives.

His lifestyle wasn't conducive to settling down or raising a family. He didn't let anyone get that close to him, and certainly not a city gal who had the same thirst for success as Mary Alice Bonner. No thanks.

He shot the last card into his cowboy hat— nothing but net. Stretching, he raked his fingers through his hair and decided Susan needed to realize that life wasn't about working yourself to death.

His parents hadn't realized that. Mary Alice hadn't, either.

Clint Scully sure as hell did.

He wasn't a saint. He liked to have money when he needed it, but what was the point if you didn't take the time to enjoy it?

As if she were having a bad dream, Alisa started to whimper. Before Clint could move, Susan awoke immediately and sat up.

"Wake up, Alisa." Susan gently took her hand and rubbed her arm. "You're having a bad dream."

Clint stood, walked over to Alisa's side and knelt on one knee.

They both helped her to sit up.

Clint reached into his pocket and handed her a red bandanna, still fairly damp from the river. "Princess, dry your eyes. It's only a dream."

She ran the bandanna over her eyes and shuddered. "I was dreaming about the accident."

Susan rubbed her back. "It's okay. You can cry if you want, Alisa."

Alisa shook her head. "I don't want to cry."

She was a tough little thing, Clint thought. She had been through so much.

"I'll get some water," he said, trying to be useful.

He walked to the buckboard where he'd put all the picnic supplies after lunch. He got three bottles of water out of the picnic basket, twisted the top off one and took a hefty sip.

He went over to the horses and absentmindedly petted one as it grazed, giving Susan some time to comfort her. His eyes never strayed from the blanket, watching as Susan hugged Alisa and got her laughing.

Susan might be a greenhorn in a lot of ways, but she was a pro when it came to dealing with a little girl with leg braces and crutches.

Yet, he'd bet all the money that he'd invested with Cletus the Clown that Susan had a disabled friend or relative.

He heard a scream, then another. He dropped the bottles of water. The adrenaline began to pump through his veins, and in a split second he sprinted back to the blanket as fast as his legs would move.

He scanned the area for trouble. When he got to the blanket, he dropped to his knees, searching for the threat that made Susan and Alisa scream, searching their faces.

Just like he did in the arena, he would put his body between them and any harm. Nothing would hurt them as long as he still had a breath in him.

But they were laughing. Laughing and screaming.

"What the…?" He breathed several sighs of relief.

Susan looked up at him. "Sorry if we alarmed you, Clint, we were just doing a little primal therapy. But thanks for coming to our rescue." She turned to Alisa. "He's just like a knight in shining armor, isn't he?"

"Well, Alisa *is* the Princess of the Gold Buckle Ranch," Clint said, forcing himself to take deep breaths to calm down. "Speaking of which, I think we ought to get back."

Susan nodded. "I have to meet with Emily."

She stood and tugged at her tank top and smoothed the legs of her warm-up pants. Her hair was damp and tangled, her jacket crumpled, but Clint thought that she'd never looked more beautiful.

They waited as Alisa put her shoes and socks on. Susan helped her with her braces, then Clint lifted her up and held on to her as she steadied herself.

"How about a Clint Scully piggy-back ride to the wagon?" he asked Alisa.

"Sure!"

Susan picked up Alisa's crutches, grabbed the blanket, umbrella and chair, and they all headed back to the wagon.

Clint hated to see their picnic end. He enjoyed their company. He'd have to think of something else the three of them could do together. Maybe a trip to town.

But first, he aimed to find time to be alone with Susan.

Emily, Clint and Susan walked toward a long, low building not far from the dining hall. Susan read the lettering on each of the doors: Medical Office, Canteen, Staff Training, Arts and Crafts and Chapel.

Emily unlocked the door to the arts and crafts room and pulled up the shade, letting in the late afternoon sun.

Susan noticed a desk in the front and built-in cabinets around the room. In the middle were two rows of three tables with chairs. The tables were covered with thick white paper.

"Go ahead. Look around," Emily said. "See what you think."

Susan took a walk around the room, opening cabinet doors and drawers, her mind ticking off what she could use.

Susan noticed dozens of boxes of crayons that had never been opened and even more watercolor paint kits. Perfect.

"I thought we could have a contest," Susan said. "Instead of me coming up with a logo, the campers could design one and put it on a T-shirt. The best one wins, and we can make it the official logo for all our merchandise."

Emily grinned. "What a great idea, Susan! I never thought of that."

"We could sketch it out on paper, then on practice fabric. They can paint it and then they can put the final design on a T-shirt. Then what?" Susan paced, brainstorming. She needed more activities to keep them occupied.

"You could make pot holders, too," Emily suggested. "We have hundreds of bags of loops and looms that were donated. It's all in the closet over there." She pointed to the left of the room.

Pot holders? She didn't know how to make pot

holders, but she was sure she could find someone at the Gold Buckle who could teach her.

"They could give a pot holder to their mothers," Clint suggested.

"Oh? Men don't cook?" Susan shot over her shoulder.

"Or they could give one to their fathers," he quickly added.

Susan looked around the room. "Maybe we could make mobiles or wall hangings of things that could be found in the forest—dried flowers, pinecones, things like that."

Emily nodded. "I knew you'd have wonderful ideas."

Susan laughed. Maybe this really was going to be fun. "I'm glad one of us thought that."

"Thank you again for volunteering." Emily gave her a big hug. "Your first class starts on Monday. Two o'clock in the afternoon, and another at four. The earlier class will have our younger kids in it. The rest of the week, you'll have the same schedule." She pulled out a piece of paper from her pocket and handed it to Susan. "Here's the list of campers and the times they are assigned. Clint will be on hand to help you. Okay, Clint?"

"Right."

"Good. That's settled."

Susan had ideas going through her mind about

other projects, but right now she wanted to ask
Emily some questions of her own.

"Emily, what's wrong with Alisa?" she blurted.

If Alisa's condition was terminal, she couldn't
deal with it. It'd be like losing her sister all over
again.

Embarrassed, Susan waved the air with her
hand, as if erasing the question. "Um…never
mind. Sorry. Forget I asked."

Emily motioned for her to take a chair. Clint sat
down next to her.

"We have a policy at the Gold Buckle Ranch
that all volunteers are briefed on every camper by
our resident doctor, Dr. Mike Trotter. Since Alisa
just arrived the other day and her situation is a
little different, Mike hasn't had a chance to review
her file yet."

"So we'll wait for Dr. Trotter," Susan said,
relieved.

"Hang on, Susan." Clint turned to her. "Let's
find out what we're dealing with here. Together,
we can figure out how to help her."

We?

He was obviously thinking that they shared a
partnership. Susan didn't know if she liked that.
Lust was one thing, being a couple was another.

Emily looked from Clint to Susan, and her gaze
settled on Susan. "Alisa did have some injuries

from the accident, but she's healed from those. She actually has a rare disease of the hip."

"Will she improve with the braces?" Clint asked.

"They've helped. But Alisa has what's called Legg-Calvé-Perthes Disease. I wish I understood it completely, but the ball of the hip fractures because of lack of blood flow. It can be treated, but she needs an operation—an osteotomy. Her doctors have been waiting until she got a little older, but apparently, now the time is right."

"Thank goodness." Susan squeezed Clint's hand, feeling relief swirling around her like the whirlpool back at the river.

"Will she be able to walk without crutches and braces?" Clint asked.

"If the operation is a success, she will," Emily said. "And I've been told that the operation is not really involved—four days in the hospital, then maybe casting, or maybe not, and then physical therapy, and she'll be walking fine. So hopefully the operation will be successful."

Susan let out the breath she'd been holding. "She's been through so much."

"And there's going to be more for her to handle." Emily met Susan's gaze. "Alisa's only temporarily with me until she can be placed with a foster family or if she's adopted."

"Alisa did tell us that she was waiting to be

adopted, but she said that her foster parents are on vacation," Clint said.

"They are, but those foster parents aren't taking her back. They just told her social worker that this morning. Alisa doesn't know yet."

Susan shook her head. "And it'll be hard for Children's Services to find an adoptive couple for a child on crutches who is facing surgery."

"Sounds like you know," Emily said.

"I do." She didn't want to expound further.

"Perhaps after the operation, it'll be easier to place her," Emily said.

Susan didn't like to hear that. "Any prospective parents worth anything would see past Alisa's crutches and braces and love her for the wonderful, sweet girl she is."

"I strongly second that," Clint added.

Emily looked at Susan, then Clint, and then stayed focused on Clint this time. "She needs parents who'll love her like she deserves to be loved. Parents who'll make her the center of their universe."

"Absolutely. You'll see to it that she gets just those kind of parents, won't you, Mrs. D?" Clint asked.

"I'm afraid it won't be up to me. It'll be up to Children's Services of the State of Wyoming."

"You'll have input, won't you?" Susan asked hopefully.

"Well, I probably won't be able to keep my

opinions to myself." Emily checked her watch and stood. "Any more questions?"

"I think you answered everything we were wondering about, Mrs. D," Clint said.

"Thanks, Emily," Susan added.

"If you think of anything else, you know where to find me." Emily handed her a key. "Would you mind locking up when you're done?"

Now that Susan's mind was at peace concerning Alisa's condition, she began to worry that Alisa wouldn't find good parents to adopt her.

But that was none of her concern. She'd be out of Alisa's life in a few more days.

She studied Clint. She wasn't going to get involved in his life, either. The last thing she wanted—or needed—was a fly-by-night man. Her father had that disease.

She just wished she could get him out of her system.

There was a fine line between life and death, health and sickness, loving someone and then never seeing them again. Susan vowed never to cross that line again.

They sat in the room in silence, each one thinking about what they'd just discovered about Alisa and the problems facing her.

Clint had the sudden urge to put on a pair of

shorts and go for a ten-mile run. Or find a rodeo and release some of his energy fighting bulls. Maybe he could do some of that screaming that Susan and Alisa seemed to be fond of.

He'd do anything to stop looking at the slump in Susan's shoulders or the bow of her head. Where was his tornado of a New Yorker? He never thought he'd want that woman over this one.

"Talk to me," he said, pulling out a chair opposite her.

Silence.

"Talk to me," he repeated. "Emily laid out some heavy stuff just now. I know how fond you are of Alisa and—"

"Aren't you?"

"You bet, but there's nothing much we can do other than to show her a good time like we did today."

"You're right. Neither of us is in a position to adopt her."

"Hell, no," Clint said. "It hadn't even crossed my mind." He certainly didn't have anything to offer the little girl.

"I can't adopt her," Susan said. "It's impossible. I have a business to run. I couldn't give her the attention she deserves, and what if...?" She shot the words out, rapid-fire.

"Whoa. Hold on just a minute. You don't have

to justify why you can't adopt her to me. I'm not the family court judge. Besides, we haven't known her very long. She could be an ax murderer or something."

That got a chuckle out of her. "You're right. I just wish that the absolute perfect couple would adopt Alisa."

"She needs two people who will be there when she comes home from school, help her with homework and tuck her in at night," he said. "Then there's carpooling to Girl Scouts, and piano lessons and PTO meetings."

Susan sighed. "Well, that sure isn't me. I'm at my office day and night."

"Doesn't fit me, either," Clint added. "I'm driving around working the rodeos."

"Well, that's decided. Neither of us has anything to offer her."

Clint nodded. "End of story."

"Okay." She looked a little sad in a way. Then Susan the businesswoman reappeared. "I might as well start getting organized for my classes." She pulled out her planner. "I need to break down my class projects by age groups, now that I know I'll have two classes." She paused with pen in hand, as if she were thinking.

Something in the back of the room caught her attention.

"Is that a phone?" She looked at him with a big grin and eyes brighter than a lighthouse beacon. "A real phone?"

"Uh-oh," Clint muttered, watching her hurry to the back of the room.

She picked up the phone and held it to her ear. "It works. Yes!"

"Darn," he mumbled.

She punched in a bunch of numbers as fast as her fingers would move. "I'll charge this to my phone card."

He got up to leave.

"Bev, it's Susan. Yes. I'm okay. How are things there? Tell me everything."

He'd gotten his wish. The feisty New Yorker was back and running her company from Mountain Springs, Wyoming.

"Susan, tell me everything!" Bev said. "Any good-looking cowboys there?"

Susan laughed. "Several, but there's one in particular."

"Tell me about him."

"His name is Clint, but I can't talk for long. I have a million things to do and I need your help. I want you to overnight some white T-shirts. Five dozen in various sizes."

"Why? What are you doing?" Bev asked.

"I'm teaching arts and crafts."

"You're what?"

"Long story. Oh, and, Bev, throw in a couple of cases of fabric paint, too. All colors. Oh, how about glitter paint? Kids like glitter. Oh, and some spools of rickrack, buttons, boxes of sequins—all colors of those, and whatever other notions you can think of. Oh, and needles and thread. No, the bigger needles. For kids. And throw in some needle threaders."

"Will do."

"Ship it overnight with the shirts."

"No problem. But tell me more about Clint!"

She told her about her horse ride with him, his trailer and their recent dip in the river. As she spoke, she looked out the front window and saw Clint jogging alongside the little brook that ran in front of the cabins. He was shirtless and wore a breezy pair of red running shorts. His legs were all muscle. He was tan and buff and his body already had a light sheen of sweat.

Suddenly, all her nerve endings were on fire.

"Susan, what's wrong?"

"Nothing, Bev. Nothing at all."

She hung up the phone and realized that she'd never even asked Bev about Winners Wear.

As she watched Clint disappear from sight, she realized how badly she needed to find out what it might be like to make love with a certain cowboy.

Chapter Eight

Clint jogged to Joe Watley's Silver River Ranch. Joe owned a nice chunk of northwest Wyoming about five miles down the main road from the Gold Buckle.

The path traversed woods, meadow and pasture—the same path that he, Joe and Jake had used to ride their horses, motorcycles, four-wheelers or snowmobiles between ranches.

The three of them had been friends forever, but had really become inseparable the first day of high school when they signed up for the rodeo team.

Jake had gravitated to riding bulls. Clint and Joe took to calf roping and were eventually paired together. Clint was the header, and Joe was the heeler. Collectively, the three of them had won about every high school title offered.

After they graduated, they all hit the professional circuit together. Jake won event after event in bull riding until he finally retired last year just after the Wheelchair Rodeo program began at the Gold Buckle Ranch. After he'd met Beth, Jake had decided that a gold wedding ring was better than a gold buckle.

After his folks lost the ranch, Clint went back to the circuit as a bullfighter and not a contestant because Joe had found another partner, and he didn't want to rope with anyone but Joe.

Joe stayed on the circuit a little longer. With every cent he'd won, he bought horses, bulls and steers. Now his Silver River Rodeo Company was one of the six biggest rodeo-stock suppliers in the United States.

Clint needed to talk to Joe. Jake was way too busy with the Wheelchair Rodeo and getting ready for the Gold Buckle Gang right now, and he wouldn't understand, anyway.

Joe Watley had a Mary Alice Bonner in his background, too, so he would understand completely when Clint talked about Susan Collins. Actually, Clint was hoping Joe would tell him to stay completely away from her.

He slowed down when he got to the barn, remembering his vow that there would be no ties with Susan—just a physical relationship.

The fact that she had to call her office the second she found a phone and couldn't get away from her job—not even for a few days—reinforced to him that they just didn't mesh.

So why was he thinking about her so much?

He walked around the barn, stopping for some small talk with the hands and admiring the horses. He paused for a drink and a soak from the hose that hung on a small outbuilding.

"Well, look what the cat dragged in."

Clint looked up to see the big outline of Joe Watley in the doorway of the barn.

"Hey, cowboy." Clint wiped his hands on his shorts and held one out.

Joe had a strong and meaty grip. He'd gained about fifty pounds since their calf-roping days, all of it pure muscle.

"What brings you by? It's too late for lunch and too early for supper. You must want to check on your investments."

Clint co-owned a couple dozen bulls, broncs and steers with Joe, most of it rodeo rough stock, along with dozens of fine quarter horses, but he let Joe handle the business end. Clint wrote him checks, Joe bought the stock, and eventually wrote bigger checks back to Clint.

Being a partner with Joe Watley was like having a gold mine in the backyard.

"I came for a cold one, and maybe some talk, but first the cold one. Make mine water. I'm on duty tonight at the dining hall and then at the nightly movie."

They walked to the ranch house, a sprawling rustic log home with walls of windows that overlooked the mountains and Joe's kingdom. It was spotless inside, thanks to Joe's housekeeper and all-around warden, Aunt Maggie.

Clint took a seat on one of the rocking chairs on the porch as his friend went inside. He returned with four bottles of water, and handed two to Clint.

Clint nodded his thanks.

"Glad you showed up. You can help me load the horses that I'm loaning to the Gold Buckle Gang."

"No problem."

Joe took a long draw of water. "I'll be there Monday morning. I'm doing two trail rides, one in the morning and one after lunch. I've been looking forward to it."

Clint nodded.

"Are you going to keep me guessing or are you going to tell me what you want to talk about?"

Clint took a long drink then poured some water down the back of his neck.

Joe rubbed his chin. "She must be pretty special for Cheyenne Clint Scully to go to the trouble of running up here."

Clint grinned. "All right, all right. Her name is Susan Collins, and she's a workaholic from New York City."

"New York City?" Joe gave a long whistle. "She's a long way from home."

"Yeah. She has her own company there. Sounds like a big deal. She calls it Winners Wear."

Joe shook his head. "She's a workaholic, and you're a country cowboy. Sounds like a match made in heaven."

Clint swore and shrugged. "There's no match, Joe. She's heading back to New York in a week. I think we're just going to end up slaking a little mutual lust in the meantime. End of story."

"Then what are you doing sitting here drinking water and looking at my ugly face when you could be slaking your lust?"

Clint laughed. He liked Joe's sense of humor and liked his advice, advice he gave whether or not you wanted to hear it.

Clint stood and stretched. "You know, you're right. Time is wasting. Let's go load the horses."

"Hold on a minute, cowboy."

"Yeah?"

"It's written all over your face." Joe gave him an easy punch on the arm. "You've gone and fallen for an ambitious gal, haven't you?"

Clint almost choked on the water. "I have three words to say to you, pal—Mary Alice Bonner."

"That was decades ago, Clint. Aren't you over her yet?"

"It was just *two* years ago, *cowboy*." Clint could still feel the anger and disappointment that he'd felt that morning when he read Mary Alice's note. "I'm over her, but that doesn't mean I haven't learned from my mistakes. Unlike you."

"Why are you bringing Ellen Rogers up?" Joe asked, with a white-knuckled grip on the porch railing.

"They're all cut from the same cloth. Believe me. They have the same ambition and drive." Clint shook his head. "City and country just don't mix, Joe."

Joe shrugged. "Maybe you're right. But maybe you should give her a chance. You might be missing out on a good thing. Obviously, she made a big impression on you in a very short time. Has any other woman ever done that?"

Clint grunted, tossed the empty plastic bottles of water on the rocker and vaulted over the railing of the porch. "Maybe you're right."

Before Clint could take a step, he felt a tug on

his arm as Joe yanked him back. They stood nose-to-nose, jogging shoes to boots as Joe got in his face.

"What is big, tough bullfighter Cheyenne Clint really scared of? Certainly not a woman. You've had more buckle bunnies than eight cowboys could handle."

He fisted his hands in Joe's shirt and a button went flying. "Susan's not a buckle bunny. There's just something about her. I don't know, Joe. She's got me all knotted up."

"Woo-ee. I can't believe this is Cheyenne Clint talking." He broke into a big grin. "What else is going on in that thick skull of yours?"

Clint let go of Joe's shirt, picked up Joe's shirt button from the dirt and handed it to him. "There's a little girl, too."

"She has a daughter?"

"No, a little orphan that the Dixons are looking after until she's adopted."

"And you're thinking of hanging up your spurs and adopting her? With Susan?"

"It crossed my mind. Or maybe they'd let me adopt her by myself. I have enough money, that'll work in my favor. But it's too premature for a big decision like that, Joe."

His friend gave a long, low whistle. "Take your time thinking about that, partner. That's a big responsibility, adopting a little girl by yourself. And you can't drag her around to rodeos and bull ridings with you."

"I know. I've visited a lot of hospitals, Joe, and been around a lot of children, but no kid has grabbed my heart more than Alisa."

"All I can say is look at Jake. I've never seen him so happy since he met Beth. Who would have thought he'd get married? But he hung up his spurs and never looked back. It can be done, Clint. But give it more time."

"I know." Clint nodded. "I suppose there are worse things than settling down, huh?"

"Like *not* grabbing on to the best thing in your life and *not* going after her," Joe said.

"Can I join you?" Clint asked.

He placed his orange plastic tray on the table next to Susan's. A mountain of spaghetti and meatballs covered the plate. A huge salad and a piece of chocolate cake topped off the tray.

"Sure." Susan had been waiting and watching for him. Then finally he'd walked into the dining hall looking freshly showered and shaved and surrounded by a bunch of girls and boys. He laughed and joked with them, signed autographs, admired cowboy hats and tipped his own hat to the girls.

The girls giggled and swooned when he did

that. They weren't immune to his charms any more than she was.

There was a sincerity and lightness about Clint that made a person feel better by just being with him. There would be no strings attached if a woman had a fling with Clint Scully, and that just suited her fine. She didn't want any strings, either.

He took a seat on the bench. "You're all alone?"

She nodded. "I needed some quiet time after this afternoon."

He raised an eyebrow. "What happened? You okay?"

"Physically, I'm fine. Mentally, I'm not sure I'll ever recover." She took a bite of a meatball. "Beth Dixon asked me to help get a gaggle of girls settled into cabin A. It was loud. Screaming, yelling, giggling. The mandatory pillow fight." She rubbed her forehead and pinched her nose in an exaggerated motion. "They put on enough makeup to paint the Empire State Building and sprayed enough perfume to kill the ozone twice."

"Ouch. How long did you have to watch them?"

"For about eight minutes."

Clint chuckled. "Then you deserve a nice, relaxing dinner."

"What's the movie tonight?" she asked, thinking that she might watch it.

"Something with John Wayne in it."

"I'll pass. Maybe I can find a book to read. I haven't had time to read in years."

Clint had the tiniest bit of sauce at the corner of his mouth. She wanted to reach over and just wipe it off with her finger. Or lick it off with her tongue.

She stared at it, then at the side of his jaw and the smooth, tanned skin of his neck. He smelled like peppermint soap, pine and maybe a little starch, probably from his fresh-from-the-package shirt that sported the usual crease marks.

She didn't have much time left at the Gold Buckle. And she intended to make the most of it.

With Clint.

Emily motioned for Susan to sit beside her in the front row of the converted dining room. On the stage, a mix of people set up music stands and tuned up their instruments for a sing-along. Several cowboys were putting together a set of drums. Two others were testing the microphone.

Emily and Susan made small talk, mostly about how Jake started Wheelchair Rodeo, and how they expanded to their current program, the Gold Buckle Gang. They wanted to add yet another program to reach out to troubled kids.

Susan could tell that Emily had something else on her mind.

"I need to talk to you about Alisa," Emily finally said.

She took a deep breath and met Emily's gaze. "Is she all right?"

"She's fine." Emily patted her hand. "Calm down. I'm not going about this the right way. It's just that Alisa has been talking about you and Clint nonstop since yesterday, and I thought you could help her deal with something. I think it's going to be very difficult for her."

"Is it medical? I have money, Emily. I'll pay for whatever she needs. Don't wait for Children's Services if Alisa needs the operation right away."

Emily patted her hand. "It's nothing like that, at least not now. I just found out that there's a couple coming out tonight with Alisa's adoption worker, and Alisa wants to talk to you about it. Dex and I talked to her, as did her worker, but she wants to talk to you. She said you had a sister that's in heaven just like her parents and would know how she feels. Would you mind just spending a few minutes with her? Her social worker told her that she wouldn't be going back to her foster parents, and I think she's afraid of another rejection from this couple."

"Emily, surely there is someone else more qualified than I am to talk to Alisa about such an important matter." She gestured toward Clint, who was talking to someone by the stage. "Even Clint is more natural with kids than I am."

"I suggested Doc Trotter and the child psychiatrist we have on staff, but she wants you because she has found something in you that she likes. There's something about you she trusts, and that's very special to a child."

"I'm flattered. I mean…oh, Emily, if you only knew—" Tears stung Susan's eyes.

While she wanted Alisa to have parents who loved her, they had to be special people, because Alisa was a very special girl with special needs.

Special. What exactly did that mean, anyway?

It meant two people who could put a child first, put her needs above theirs and form a family, accept her and make her happy. Above all, they'd love her and wouldn't leave when things got tough and never come back like Susan's own father had.

Susan would be leaving soon. It wouldn't do for the girl to get even more attached to her.

Who was she kidding? She herself was attached to Alisa.

She looked into Emily's kind eyes. How could she say no?

"I'll do what I can, Emily."

"Thank you. She's a sweetheart, isn't she?"

"She is."

"I'd adopt her myself, but she needs a younger couple than Dex and I."

Susan put her hand on Emily's arm and whispered, "Here she comes now."

Susan waved to Alisa, who was walking toward them. Suddenly Emily got up from her chair, babbling something about having to get ready for her guests.

Emily smoothed Alisa's hair. Her hair didn't need smoothing, but Emily clearly had great affection for the girl.

"Remember, Alisa, after the sing-along come right home."

"I'll remember, Mrs. Dixon." Alisa's eyes lost their glow. "But what if I don't like them?"

Emily made a fist like a hitchhiker and pointed her thumb toward the door. "Then we'll kick them right out."

Alisa giggled uneasily, then turned to Susan. "I'm meeting two people who might adopt me."

Susan nodded and put a hand on Alisa's shoulder. She didn't know what else to do, or say.

"Mrs. Dixon, can Susan and Cheyenne Clint come with me and meet them?"

"This is really none of my business or Clint's, sweetie," Susan said. "It's between you and your adoption worker. But if you need to talk, I'm listening."

Alisa nodded, but she seemed boneless and slumped into the chair awkwardly. Luckily, Clint walked out onstage and started talking on the microphone, and she perked right up.

Emily gave Alisa a little pat on the head, raised her eyebrows and thinned her lips to Susan with a "this is going to be difficult" expression on her face, and left.

Clint sat down, strummed his guitar, and Susan watched Alisa's sweet face fill up with the excitement that she'd lost earlier.

Clint played the guitar and sang like an actual country and western star. He even looked the part, with his guitar slung over his shoulders and his cowboy hat shading his eyes.

Susan felt a rising uneasiness. Alisa was getting too fond of her, and Susan was worried that Alisa wouldn't give any adoption prospects a fair chance.

Alisa slipped her little hand into hers. Susan tried to relax and think of how to give her a gentle push toward the couple that she'd be meeting tonight.

To stop herself from obsessing about Alisa, Susan tried to listen to the words as Clint sang "Home on the Range."

It didn't seem like the corny song that she'd heard millions of times. It was a song about hearth and home and roots, feeling connected, and yet insignificant, to the wonder of nature.

He poured his heart and soul into each word.

But what did the words mean to Clint? He had a ranch that he didn't even run. He didn't stay in any one place for too long. Did he secretly long for roots of his own?

The song ended and the audience was silent until the last chord of his guitar faded along with the last note of his deep voice. Then they broke out into hoots, whistles and loud applause. Clint took a bow and waved his hat, setting the teen girls to screaming. With a bemused glance at Susan, he laughed.

Clint caught up with them later outside the dining hall, where they were slowly walking to the Dixons' house. "You ladies aren't staying for the John Wayne movie?"

Alisa shook her head. "I have to meet some people who might adopt me. Will you both come with me? Please? Please?"

Clint must have caught the desperation in Alisa's voice. "What's got you so nervous, Princess?"

"I don't want to meet them. What if I don't like them?"

"What if you do?" Susan bent down and took her hands. "Wouldn't it be awesome?"

In the outside lighting, Susan could see a single tear slowly trail down Alisa's cheek.

"I want to go to the movie instead," Alisa said softly.

Susan wiped the tear off the girl's cheek with a finger. She felt like crying herself. "You can watch John Wayne any old time. Go and meet the people. They came all the way here to see you, so right away they think you're special. I think you should give them a chance."

Susan smiled in spite of the sadness clutching her heart. She wanted to wrap Alisa in her arms and not let anything hurt her.

"Remember what Emily said?" Susan made the same hitchhiker pose as Emily had earlier. "If you don't like them, you can boot them out. But I'll bet they'll be terrific."

Alisa sniffed. "Okay, Susan."

"How about a lift, Alisa?" Clint asked.

"I'm okay."

"I know you're okay, but how about a lift anyway?"

She wiped more tears away with the hem of her sweatshirt. "I'd like that, Cheyenne Clint."

Clint squatted down. "Hop on."

Susan took her crutches and helped Alisa onto Clint's back. They walked toward the back of the Dixons' residence where there was a separate entrance to their kitchen.

Along the way, Clint cracked jokes and got Alisa laughing. It struck Susan that this was how she'd always wanted her family to be. She remembered longing to take walks with her parents, laughing with them and wanting to go on a picnic. She'd hated that her mother was always working or her father was always gone.

Just once, she'd wanted to see her father hoist Elaine on his back, and make her feel like a part of the family, not a bothersome burden.

Above all, she'd always wanted him to make Elaine laugh so she'd forget her troubles, if only for a little while.

She was attracted to Clint, and the more she got to know him, the more she liked him.

She needed to stop her brain from working double time, filling her mind with thoughts of Alisa, Clint and her own lonely life.

She should be thinking of production schedules, filling orders, packaging and shipping.

She loved the lights and hustle of the city, but Clint was pure country. She was a workaholic, and Clint's pulse barely registered.

He was fabulous with children, but it was Susan that Alisa wanted to talk to.

She was making herself dizzy.

They reached the main house and a tall, muscular man dressed in the cowboy fashion with twinkling eyes and a big smile answered Clint's knock.

"Howdy, Clint." He grasped Clint's hand in a meaty shake, then his gaze dropped to Alisa.

"Well, about time you got home, Cinderella!" He smiled at Susan, then grabbed her hand and started pumping away.

"Susan Collins," she said.

"I'm Dex Dixon, and I'm the foreman of this outfit, but only when my wife lets me be."

He stepped out onto the porch and held the door open for Alisa to have more room to walk through. "Your company's here, Alisa, and they seem like really nice folks."

"Okay," she said in a shaky, thin voice. Alisa turned to Susan and Clint. "Thanks."

"You're welcome, Princess."

Alisa held her arms up, and Susan knew exactly what she wanted. A hug.

Crouching down, she waited as Alisa took a wobbly step and wrapped her arms around Susan's neck.

Susan couldn't help herself. She wrapped her arms around the thin, tiny girl and felt herself free-falling through space and time. She had a gut-wrenching need to protect the sweet, sad Alisa, a child that she barely knew, but who was so like Elaine.

Susan also wanted to look over the two people waiting inside for Alisa, but she didn't have any right.

Clint removed his hat and held it over his heart.

"You'll be absolutely fine, Princess Alisa of the Gold Buckle Ranch."

Alisa giggled, and when she walked away, she had the air of actual royalty ready to grant an audience.

Susan looked at Clint and sighed.

"I know," he said, slapping his hat back on his head. "Maybe we can help her—together."

Chapter Nine

Clint walked Susan to her cabin after dropping Alisa off at the Dixons'.

"I'm worried about Alisa going through the whole adoption process," Susan said.

"Me, too. But she's strong. My money's on her."

He'd met a lot of kids over the years. Many of them touched his heart, and many of them had him blinking back tears, but something about Alisa made him want to take her home, protect her and never let her out of his sight.

He'd been thinking about his conversation with Joe. If he were married, or had a steady job, he'd seriously think about adopting Alisa himself. He didn't think he was actually falling for Susan; all he knew was that something about her got his blood pumping and turned his breathing irregular. When she touched him like she did in the river, he was ready to explode.

Marriage. He didn't want to go down that trail again. He was a bullfighter and an adrenaline junkie. His primary home was a trailer. Mary Alice Bonner knew that, and she headed for Chicago. Susan Collins had no idea what his life was actually like.

"A penny for your thoughts," Susan said, stopping in front of her cabin.

"I'm thinking that I have to get back to the movie," he lied. "Would you mind if I came by later? I'll bring wine."

"I'd like that. See you in a couple of hours."

Checking his watch, he saw that he had about ten minutes before he had to be on duty at the movie. He walked to the dining hall, grabbed a bottle of water made a little small talk with one of the nurses who cornered him, and slipped out the side door.

He walked back to the Dixons' ranch house, not exactly knowing what bothered him. He just wanted to check on things.

The lights were on and the curtains weren't closed. He could easily see into their living room.

Dex and Emily sat on a brown leather love seat. Alisa sat on a kid-size rocking chair. Her crutches leaned against a coffee table. On the couch sat a middle-aged, impeccably groomed couple holding hands. Another serious-looking woman in a somber gray pantsuit studied a folder on her lap. Clint assumed that she was Alisa's adoption worker.

The couple looked nice enough, he supposed. They were dressed like they had enough money to give Alisa whatever she wanted. He looked at the car parked in front, a brand-new silver-gray BMW. That had to belong to the couple. It certainly wasn't Dex Dixon's car.

Upper-class yuppies. Not bad.

Clint moved back into the shadows when he heard a twig snap. He saw her silhouette even before he smelled her floral scent: Susan.

She stopped in front of the Dixons' living room and looked in. She tried to be casual and studied her nails, not that she could see them in the dark.

He didn't know how he could make his presence known without scaring her.

He cleared his throat. She jumped and began to run.

"Susan, it's me." He grabbed her arm, and she took a swing at him. He ducked and dodged. Nice defensive reflexes. Good for her. "Susan, it's Clint."

She stopped in midswing. "You scared me to death. What the hell are you doing out here?"

He let go of her arm but held on to her hand. "Same thing you are. Spying."

She grinned and they both turned to look at the people talking in the living room. Alisa was smiling and laughing.

"She looks happy. Doesn't she?" Susan asked.

"Yeah. I figure that's the prospective parents' Beemer over there."

She looked at the car, then stared back at the house. "They look nice." Susan sighed. "I wonder what they're like."

"I'm sure Alisa will let us know."

They both watched as the woman handed Alisa a present. "Oh, brother," Susan complained. "Nothing like stacking the deck."

Clint made a grunting sound. "The nerve of some people."

"It's probably a doll. Don't they know she's too old for dolls?"

They both waited to see what the gift would be.

"A CD player." Susan let out a puff of air. "Sheesh."

"And some CDs. Look at her grin. She likes them."

"She likes Disney songs."

"I know."

It felt natural to be with Susan, holding her hand, staring into someone's house. Strange, but natural. They shared a bond between them—concern over a young girl.

"Had enough?" he asked.

"Yes. I just wanted to make sure she was doing okay."

He gave her hand a little squeeze, and she smiled up at him.

That was his undoing. He slipped his other hand around her waist and pulled her to him. She looked beautiful in the moonlight with her big eyes twinkling.

He gave her a second or two to push him away or tell him no, and when she didn't, he kissed her—lightly at first. He lifted his head and smiled. She smiled back.

He kissed her again.

She pulled her hand from his and wrapped her arms around his neck. He fisted his hand in her soft hair, hair that glimmered in the moonlight, and moved her head to give him more access to her lips.

He rubbed her back. She kneaded his neck with her fingers.

He broke the kiss to gather his wits about him before he pulled her down to the gravel and dispensed with her clothes.

They stood forehead-to-forehead, smiling, shuffling to a soundless rhythm.

His hand moved naturally to her waist. They swayed, barely moving. He inhaled her scent, kissed her lightly on the forehead. She put her hand on his cheek, then moved her hands across his shoulders and smiled up at him.

He hadn't felt this good in a long time.

"Clint?"

"Hmm?"

"Don't you have to go to the John Wayne movie?" Her voice was barely a whisper, and it held a touch of regret.

"Shoot." He'd forgotten. "I'd better make tracks."

With a look back, they saw that Alisa was still laughing. Hand in hand, he and Susan walked in the direction of the dining hall.

"I can make it to my cabin alone," Susan said. "You go ahead."

"Still up for that wine later?" he asked.

"Sure."

Her sexy smile made him think of star-filled Wyoming nights and warm summer breezes as they whispered through the pines and meadows. That's when he really felt alive.

He wanted her, and time was running out.

Susan jumped in the shower, then slipped into a pair of pink sweats. She settled into a chair with her planner to wait for Clint, needing something to do to take her mind off him.

She wanted to see him again. She had already decided he wasn't her type, and he certainly wasn't the kind of guy to get serious over. Yet she couldn't help herself.

She had no doubt that he was interested in a sexual relationship. He knew that she'd be gone by the end of the week, so there would be no surprises there. Susan wanted him, too. She'd make it clear that their relationship couldn't go any further.

She was a modern woman, and he was an attractive man. What was the harm in some good, healthy sex?

Then they'd go their separate ways. No strings attached.

To take her mind off Clint, she unzipped her planner. This evening, she actually had to look for where she'd put it. Back home, it never left her hand. She had it stuffed with pieces of paper and other junk, and Bev always joked that some day Susan would have to have it surgically removed.

She jotted down some notes for her upcoming art classes, thinking the kids might enjoy learning how the shirts they were going to sew and decorate were made.

After the designing and decorating was done, they could vote for their favorite T-shirt. She'd give out prizes for the winners and finalists. Maybe certificates to the canteen, if Emily was willing.

It grew chilly in the room, so she decided to start a fire in the fireplace. A fire was always romantic. She twisted paper, piled up kindling, then stacked on a couple of logs. She struck a match and watched the paper catch on fire. Okay, it wasn't exactly a blaze, but it had potential. She threw on more kindling, blew on the flames and watched them grow hotter.

She washed her hands, pulled out two water glasses for the wine and set them on the counter. She peeked out the front window again, but saw nothing but darkness beyond the glow of the porch light.

She actually found herself whistling, and she never whistled.

She picked up the book that she'd signed out of the library in the lobby. "Mmm…a real book." It would be a luxury to be able to read something other than printouts of sales figures, supply catalogs or invoices. She tucked her feet under her and began to read.

Three chapters later there was a knock on the door.

"Yes?"

"It's Clint."

Immediately, her heart started to beat faster, and she felt a nervous excitement bubbling inside her.

When she opened the door and saw all sorts of bugs flying around the porch light, she yanked Clint in by an arm and slammed the door shut behind him.

He let out a short, sharp whistle and made a show out of returning the crease to his shirt sleeves. "Just couldn't wait to get your hands on me, huh?"

"Didn't want to let any bugs in."

"Ouch." He patted his heart. "You really know how to hurt a guy."

When she turned toward him, his eyes were scanning her body.

"You're a sight for tired eyes, Susan."

"Your tired eyes just saw me a couple of hours ago."

"But that's what John Wayne always says."

"What does Clint Scully always say?"

He rubbed his chin, as if thinking. "He's a polite cowboy. He always asks a lady for a kiss."

"Hmm…maybe I should play hard to get."

"No, don't."

He closed the distance between them and wrapped her in his arms. His hand cut through her hair and cupped the back of her neck. Just before his mouth moved over hers, Susan held him back.

"Where is this going to go, Clint?"

"I think you know. If you've got a problem with that, you might as well let me know now."

"Just sex? No commitment?"

"You're leaving at the end of the week to go back to New York. My life is here, or on the road. How much commitment can we have?"

For some reason, when he said it, it seemed so shallow, but she wanted him, there was no denying that. "Kiss me, cowboy."

He did, and she felt his kiss down to her toes. Before her knees buckled, he lifted her off her feet.

Walking several steps to the couch, he sat down with her on his lap.

Clint wiped his face with a red bandanna that he pulled out of his pocket. "Did you start that fire?"

She nodded.

"Nice job. Sure is hot in here. Where did you learn how to start a fire, city slicker?"

"My grandmother's house had a fireplace."

He kissed her again. Her head rested on the arm of the sofa, and his hand started to travel under the hem of her sweatshirt.

She reached for his shirt. With a few tugs on

the snaps, it popped open. She ran her palms over his strong, tanned chest. His scars were there, and she traced kisses down one of them, as if she could erase it.

He looked down at her, and let out a noise that was half breath and half whistle. His hand splayed across her stomach, moved up her midriff and cupped a breast.

"You're beautiful, Susan."

He put his feet up on the coffee table, causing her planner to drop. All the papers she had tucked inside it fell out into a big mess on the floor.

"I'm sorry," he said, moving her feet away. "Let me pick that up."

"That's okay, Clint. Leave it."

But it was too late. He had the picture of Elaine in his hand, the one taken a month before she died. Susan sat up and straightened her sweatshirt.

"Is this Elaine?" he asked softly.

Susan nodded. "Yes."

"She reminds me of Alisa."

"Yes. Me, too. Very much so."

"Who is she to you?" he asked softly.

"My sister."

"That explains a lot."

She raised an eyebrow. "What do you mean by that?"

"At first, you acted a little nervous around Alisa."

"I know."

He studied the picture. "Does she have an artificial leg?"

Susan suddenly couldn't talk. Nodding, she got up and walked to the kitchen. "Would you like some wine now?"

"Sure."

She thought that pouring the wine would give her a little time to calm herself and catch her breath, but not when Clint arrived at her side and helped with the corkscrew. It was nice of him to assist, but he didn't have to do it from behind with his arms around her, his warm chest on her back, his hard body moving against her behind.

He scooped up the glasses and the wine and headed back to the couch. He held out his hand, and she took it.

She had known how she wanted this evening to end, but now her mind whirled.

She didn't want to think about Elaine or Alisa; she'd been doing that enough lately. She wanted Clint Scully. She wanted to make love with him, but she didn't want to fall in love with him. If she did, it would cause too many complications and it'd hurt too much when she had to leave.

Maybe all she'd ever have would be this one time with him, and she was going to make the most of it.

The bedroom was down the hall—cheerful and

inviting, with its colorful blankets and array of plump pillows. If she led him there, she'd seem much too eager.

"Something wrong?" he asked.

"Um…no." She pointed down the hall. "The bed is more comfortable. We can talk there."

She sounded like an idiot. How obvious could she be?

He grinned. "Lead the way."

Clint sat on the edge of the bed and put the glasses on the end table, then tugged off his boots. They landed on the floor with a thump. Susan walked over to the other side of the bed.

She'd never been this nervous before. This just didn't feel right—not since Clint found the picture of Elaine.

Clint tossed his hat onto a chair. He patted the bed. "Something's bothering you. Sit back, relax and tell me about it."

Silence. She didn't want to talk. She just wanted to forget.

She slid off her sandals and sat cross-legged on the bed next to him.

He put his hand over hers and played with her fingers. "Tell me about Elaine."

For a while, she couldn't catch her breath. "I…uh…I don't think I can."

"I could tell the way you handled Alisa's braces

by the river that you knew what you were doing. Elaine wore braces, didn't she?"

Susan felt the sting of tears when Clint said her sister's name.

She took a deep breath and let it out slowly. "Elaine had bone cancer. She died when she was nine, a couple of years older than Alisa. I was twelve. I did everything I could, Clint, but…" She stopped to find her voice.

He took her hand and sandwiched it between his. "Her death must have hurt you," he said softly, gently. His sincere blue eyes showed his concern.

She'd thought of the day that Elaine died a thousand times. Her father was summoned home from Bermuda, where he was leading another tour, and he and her mother had each held one of Elaine's hands. Susan could only stand at the end of the bed and cry, knowing that Elaine knew that she was there.

Elaine had given her a weak smile. "I'll see you when you get to heaven."

"Don't go," Susan remembered sobbing. "I'll do more for you. I'll be a better sister."

But in the end, there hadn't been any time to be a better sister. Elaine had closed her eyes and the pain twisting her small features had vanished in an instant. At that moment, she had looked like a por-celain angel. Exactly like the angel her mother had put on Elaine's nightstand to watch over her. An angel that hadn't done the job it was supposed to do.

Clint didn't say a word. He just reached over, wiped a tear from her cheek.

"After she died, I went out to the railroad tracks behind our house and waited for the nine o'clock train," she said quietly. "When the train zoomed by, I screamed and screamed until I didn't have a voice left. When I got home, I found that my father had left again, but this time he wasn't coming back. He'd never even said goodbye to me."

"You lost two important people on the same night," Clint said.

She nodded. "And my mother was never the same."

Susan had never been the same, either. On that day she'd vowed she would never, ever get close to anyone again. Loving someone only meant getting hurt and ending up alone.

She sniffed. "I blamed Elaine for my father's leaving, do you know that? Poor kid. I blamed her."

"Susan, you were just a kid."

Clint pulled her into his arms. They lay on the bed together facing each other. He held her to him and rubbed her back.

"I understand. Let it out. Go ahead."

She couldn't keep the floodgates locked in place anymore, and it seemed like she'd been waiting dozens of years to let herself cry, let herself heal. Clint was offering himself to her just for that reason. So she let him. She cried like she'd never cried before.

"Seeing Alisa in the cafeteria…I don't know…it just shook me up. Thank goodness, at least there's a chance for Alisa."

"You were struggling not to get close to her, weren't you?"

"I still am. But it's impossible. She's just adorable and sweet, but I can't help but think she's latched onto us as some kind of substitute parents."

"I know. What are we going to do about that?" Clint asked.

"I don't know. I just don't know. We're going to have to talk to her eventually. Maybe the psychologist can help us."

"Excellent idea."

His eyes were so mesmerizing, and his smile so sweet, it was hard to believe that such a man existed. Throw in the fact that he had a heart of gold, and was great with children along with being a successful entrepreneur and bullfighter—well, Clint Scully was unlike any man she'd ever known.

It was a shame he didn't live in New York, but she just couldn't picture him there. She realized that she was actually going to miss him when she left. But she just wasn't going to fall in love with a man like Clint.

She had first-hand knowledge of how bitter her mother had become with an absentee husband.

She'd never allow that to happen to her.

Chapter Ten

Susan slept like she'd never slept before. No dreams. No nightmares. No ticking off long lists in her mind.

Sunshine streamed into the bedroom windows. Clint was gone—a bouquet of purple wildflowers was on the pillow next to her.

She picked it up and inhaled its scent, violets with a hint of mint.

She thought back to last night. Clint had held her tight to his warm, strong body and simply let her cry, whispering words of comfort and punctuating them with sweet kisses. He'd dried her tears and rubbed her back all through the night.

They never made love, but she had never felt more cherished.

Smiling, she held the flowers and inspected their delicate petals. After all those years struggling to keep her feelings bottled up inside her, she'd dumped them all on Clint Scully, a man she'd known only a couple of days. Go figure.

She stretched, and realized she'd never felt better in her life.

Clint helped her realize last night that she'd never let Elaine go and that she blamed herself for not doing more to help her. Susan had been only a young girl herself, and had done what she could for her sister, but in the end, it had been the decision of a higher power.

A half hour later, she was showered, dressed and walking to the dining hall thinking about a mug of steaming coffee, a plateful of scrambled eggs, fried potatoes and a bowl of cut fruit. She could eat a moose.

Emily walked out of the lobby, said a brief hello and handed her a schedule of events before she ran off. She saw her two craft classes listed for Monday and all through the week.

A rush of anticipation shot through her. Funny, she was dreading it before, but now she had a plan for the contest and some other activities, and was actually excited.

"Hi, Susan."

She looked in the direction of the voice, and saw Alisa sitting on a bench outside the lobby.

"Well, good morning. I didn't even see you there."

"I'm waiting for Mr. and Mrs. Ketchum to pick me up. They are going to take me to see their ranch. They want to adopt me."

So that was their name—the couple with the BMW.

Alisa's crutches leaned against the seat of the bench and she looked like the loneliest little girl in the world. She didn't even look happy to be going.

Susan pointed to the space next to her. "Can I wait with you?"

"Will you?" Her face brightened. "Mrs. Dixon said she'd be right back after she did a couple of things."

"Sure." Susan sat down. "So, how do you like the Ketchums?"

"They're nice. They gave me a CD player and some CDs. They weren't Disney songs, but they're okay."

Alisa lowered her eyes, and Susan suspected that

there was more to her unhappiness, and not just because she didn't receive Disney CDs. She put her arm around Alisa and hugged her close to her side.

"I'll bet you'll like their ranch, too. I'll bet they have horses and cows and, uh…whatever else is on a ranch."

"Bulls and goats," Alisa supplied.

"And maybe cats and dogs," Susan added, racking her brain to think of more ranch-related animals.

Alisa brightened at that. "Do you have any animals where you live?"

She shook her head. "I live in an apartment on the sixteenth floor in a big city. There's really no room for pets. Besides, I'm not home much to take care of them."

"That means you couldn't take care of me, either," Alisa said quietly.

Susan's heart raced at that, then sat heavy in her chest. She didn't know what to say, what to do. She had suspected that Alisa was thinking along those lines.

She had to try to make her understand without hurting her. She couldn't figure out why Alisa would want her, of all people, to adopt her. Clint, she could understand, but Alisa wanted them both.

"Why don't you give Mr. and Mrs. Ketchum a

chance? Go and see their ranch. Have fun. Just stay away from the bigger stuff like the bulls. Okay?"

Alisa gave a halfhearted smile, and that made Susan feel a little better. She hugged her, tickled her neck and she giggled.

A flash of jeans, a pale yellow shirt and a white hat caught the corner of her eye. "Here comes Clint," Susan said.

They waved and he waved back. When he got closer, he tipped his hat. "Howdy, ladies. You both look as pretty as a summer day."

He stood in front of them, looking uneasy. "Um…Alisa, Mrs. Dixon sent me here with a message for you."

He met Susan's eyes briefly, and Susan could tell that the message wasn't good.

He knelt on one knee to be eye level with Alisa. "Mr. Ketchum had to work today and sends his apologies. He won't be picking you up. Some kind of problem at work."

"Oh," Alisa said quietly. She might not have wanted to go before, but she sure looked disappointed now.

A white-hot anger bubbled inside Susan. How totally inconsiderate of Mr. Ketchum to disappoint Alisa like that. The nerve of some people. Didn't he know that she was fragile enough? And what was wrong with his wife? Couldn't she pick up Alisa?

Susan quietly seethed. She bit her lip and telegraphed her ire to Clint. He nodded. It bothered him, too.

Then it hit her. She wouldn't be any better than Mr. Ketchum. If there was some kind of crisis at the office, she'd have to stay and fix the problem.

Clint snapped his fingers. "How about a trip, ladies? I'm free until six o'clock tonight, when I'm scheduled to run the sing-along. I figure that Susan needs to see a little bit of Wyoming before she goes back to that place she calls home."

That sounded nice. She wouldn't mind Clint's company for the day. Besides, Alisa seemed to be coming out of her funk with just the mention of it.

"I'll let Emily know, and I'll be back to pick you both up."

Clint pulled his rusty truck to the front of the dining hall as Susan and Alisa came out to meet him. He hurried to the passenger side, opened the door and helped Alisa inside. "Buckle up, ladies."

Clint took the road to Joe Watley's farm.

"Is this the right way to town?" Susan asked after a while.

"No. Who said we were going to Mountain Springs?" Clint asked.

"I just assumed."

Clint grinned. "We're going to Cheyenne."

"Cheyenne what?"

"Cheyenne, Wyoming. I want you both to see my ranch."

He made a wide right turn into a field. "Hope you aren't afraid of flying," he said, heading for the small hangar.

Alisa clapped. "Awesome! I've never been in a plane before.

Susan gulped some air. "Who's flying it?"

"I am," Clint said.

"You?"

"I am. Don't worry. Cletus the Clown taught me how to fly."

She looked at him, eyes wide and mouth open.

"Just kidding," he said.

"Whose plane is it?" she asked.

"Mine. Well, actually I co-own it with Jake Dixon and Joe Watley. You know Jake, and I'll introduce you to Joe."

Clint turned off the motor and got out. He waved to Joe, who waved back. Susan scrambled out of the truck, and he handed Alisa's crutches to Susan, then helped Alisa.

"So what do you think of *Silverbird?*" he asked Alisa.

"Cool," she said.

He squatted down without saying a word, and Alisa climbed up on his back.

Susan shut the truck door and they walked to the plane. "I think I'm in the wrong business," Susan said. "Are there any openings for a rodeo clown?"

"Bullfighter." Clint grinned, introduced Joe Watley to Susan and Alisa, and settled them inside the plane as quickly as he could.

Clint was about to get into the plane, when Joe gripped his arm and chuckled. "I can see why they both have you tied up in knots, partner."

"The knots are getting tighter. I'm showing them the Lazy S."

Joe gave a long whistle. "You are serious. Have a good time."

The flight was picture-perfect—blue skies, fluffy white clouds and a bright sun. They could see for miles.

"That's the Lazy S down there." Clint pointed. "It runs from about that group of pines, follows the river, cuts over to that little outcrop of hills, and then back to where we are."

He landed with a small bump, taxied down the

runway and cut the engine. His uncle Charlie would be along soon with the pickup to collect them.

He helped them out of the plane as a series of sharp barks split the air. Rodeo, his black-and-white border collie, came bounding toward them. Alisa grabbed for his hand. Susan clutched his arm.

"He won't hurt you," Clint assured them.

He let out a shrill whistle, and Rodeo stopped in front of him, wagging his tail. He scratched the dog behind the ears and rubbed his tummy when he rolled over.

"Ladies, this is Rodeo. He herds the cows and bulls, and is better than six cowboys."

The dog licked Alisa's face, and she giggled. He sniffed at her braces and crutches, sat and looked up at her. Obviously Rodeo had found a new friend.

"I can't wait to see more of your ranch," Susan said.

That was music to his ears. That's why he'd brought them here. For some unknown reason, he wanted them to like the Lazy S.

He had a love-hate relationship with the ranch. He'd loved it growing up, and when he'd bought it back years later, he'd loved remodeling it. He painted, plastered, even decorated it himself. He bought new furniture, including a hand-carved king bed.

The house was going to be a wedding present for Mary Alice. But after she left him at the altar, he could no longer find joy in his childhood home—he just didn't want to be at the ranch anymore.

So Clint hired the best cowboys he knew to work the Lazy S, and he pretty much left them alone. Uncle Charlie lived in a small house of his own on the property and watched over everything.

The pickup appeared, but instead of Uncle Charlie, Sam Diaz, an old cowboy with a heart of gold and several gold teeth to match, welcomed them and opened the doors of the vehicle

"I'll show you my horses first," Clint said proudly. "I have some of the best quarter horses in this part of Wyoming. Then I'll show you Mighty Max, the rankest bull around. He's the one who rammed his horn through me in Reno and sidelined a couple bull riders for the year. His owner was going to put him down, but I bought him instead."

Clint showed them horse after horse, bull after bull. He put Alisa sidesaddle on a little pony and he led her around the corral. Rodeo, the border collie, walked by their side and kept looking at Alisa as if to make sure she was okay.

As Alisa enjoyed her ride, Susan looked at the expanse of meadow, the miles of fence, the mountains in the distance and the pretty pond with ducks. The main house, long and low and rambling, sat in the middle of a copse of tall trees. There were pots of flowers hanging from the porch rafters, and a three-tiered fountain in the middle of the brick walk that led to the main house.

She put her hand out and let the water flow over her palm. "I'd love to pull over a chair and listen to this water all day."

"You would?" Clint raised an eyebrow. "That seems too tame for Susan Collins, CEO."

He was right. She never would have thought of such a thing a few days ago. She wondered why now, why here. Maybe there was something to this vacation thing after all.

She knew that she'd thrown herself into her work to make it a success, but there was a price she paid—maybe too high of a price.

Clint was showing her that there was more to life than working yourself to death.

Maybe if she hadn't been such a workaholic, she might have found a husband who loved her. Maybe she would have had children. Maybe… maybe…she'd never know.

Clint tied Wanda, the little pony, to a railing and lifted Alisa off. "I'll show you the main house."

A tall, large man with a white chef's apron and a white handlebar mustache opened the door and waved in welcome.

"Ladies, this is my uncle Charlie. He's chief cook and bottle washer at the Lazy S. He's also the vet, my business manager, the head wrangler, the horse trainer, and he's very, very bossy."

Uncle Charlie took off his white cowboy hat and held it over his heart. "Welcome to the Lazy S, ladies. Your beauty dwarfs the spacious skies of Wyoming, and your smiles outshine the sun."

"He also thinks he's a poet," Clint added.

Susan smiled. "I think he's charming."

"Me, too," said Alisa.

He lumbered down the stairs and enveloped Susan in a bear hug. He smelled of garlic and tomatoes and maybe cumin.

"You must be Susan. Clint radioed me that he was bringing some guests. As luck would have it, you're all in time for my famous beef chili."

Uncle Charlie slapped his hands on his knees and leaned over. He winked at Alisa. "Is this Alisa?" He held his hand out, and Alisa slipped hers into his.

He shook it ever so gently. "Welcome to the Lazy S, darlin'. You look like a young lady who'd like a big bowl of cowboy chili and maybe an ice cream cone for dessert. Come in. Come in."

He slapped Clint's back. "About time you stopped by. You have a half-dozen messages on your desk from hospitals wanting you to stop by and entertain the kids. And the Make a Wish Foundation called. There's a boy with cancer at the Casper Hospital who's asking for you."

Clint nodded. "I'll make arrangements."

Susan stood motionless. He visited hospitals, too?

She felt Clint's hand on the small of her back. "Let me show you around."

The entranceway floor was made of large reddish-brown tiles with thick gray cement around them. The walls were varnished knotty pine, and Susan wondered if the planks had come from the nearby woods. Large pieces of furniture, heavy with wood and marble, fit perfectly with the vaulted ceilings and skylights. A floor-to-ceiling fireplace with a mantel that looked like half of a redwood tree took up most of one wall. There were windows everywhere.

"This is just beautiful, Clint. My apartment could fit into this room about ten times."

He nodded and looked around as if he was seeing it for the first time himself. "Glad you like it."

She heard the pride in his voice.

"Clint did a lot of work on the place. He's very talented," Uncle Charlie said.

Clint shifted on his feet, obviously uncomfortable at the praise. She smiled her admiration, and could have sworn that his face reddened.

When Alisa had to use the bathroom, Susan's curiosity got the best of her, and she wandered down the hall.

There were three bedrooms, all huge. Clint's was in the back. Three sides of the room held floor-to-ceiling shelves. Hundreds of trophies, pictures and belt buckles of every shape and size decorated the shelves.

Near the remaining wall was a king-size bed made out of round logs. She could picture Clint stretched out and naked, holding his hand out to her to join him. Her body heated and her cheeks flamed.

A light went on and she jumped.

"I-I'm sorry. I didn't mean to—"

Clint held up a hand. "No problem. Look all you want."

"I can't believe all your awards." She pointed to a picture. "I see you roping the little cows."

He laughed. "Those are steers."

He showed her pictures of him saving bull riders named Chris Shivers, Adriano Moraes, Paulo Crimber and dozens of others.

All the while, she tried not to look at his big, comfortable bed.

Then she suffered through pictures of him with

several Miss Rodeos, all of whom had long, fluffy hair under white hats, fringed blouses with sequins and sprayed-on jeans.

She could tell by Clint's nonstop chatter and big grin that he liked the rodeo life and was proud of what he'd accomplished. All the people in the pictures seemed like family to him.

"Every year, whatever cowboys can make it come to the Lazy S and help me with round-up. We work all day, then drink beer and eat barbecue and relive every ride and every wreck." He chuckled as he remembered something. "Good friends. Good times."

"Do they work with the kids at the Gold Buckle, too?"

"Absolutely. Some bring their families and camp out in trailers by the river. Some of the single cowboys stay all year long and work for the Dixons. When you have a cowboy for a friend, you have a friend for life."

Susan thought it would be wonderful to have friends like that. She didn't have really good friends, just business friends, and there was a difference. She was the boss, and she didn't discuss her personal life with them to any great length, not even Bev.

Yet she'd told Clint her deepest personal thoughts.

She wanted to thank him for last night, but she

had a feeling he already knew how much it had meant to her.

She remembered how he'd held her, how he'd rubbed her back, wiped her tears. His kisses were sweet and caring, his arms strong around her.

Maybe he was right about cowboys and friends.

It made her heart soar that that they were friends, and she supposed that they should leave it at that.

Sex would just mess everything up.

Wouldn't it?

Chapter Eleven

Susan could hear the phone ring in the distance. Soon Uncle Charlie yelled, "Clint, it's Emily Dixon for you."

"Excuse me," he said to Susan. "The phone's in the kitchen."

"Sure. Go ahead. I'll wait in the living room."

On her way, she listened at the bathroom door and heard Alisa singing. "Alisa, everything okay?"

"Yes."

"Okay."

Susan sat in one of the comfortable chairs in the living room. Alisa and Clint appeared at the same time.

Clint sat on the thick coffee table across from Susan and made eye contact with them both. "Mrs. D said that there was a change in the schedule. I don't have to be back today and neither does Alisa. So how would you both like to stay overnight here?"

"Really?" Alisa asked, looking at them.

Overnight at Clint's house? Susan immediately thought of joining him in his big bed. Her body came alive with excitement that she didn't know existed within her.

She tried to calm herself and sound casual. "Sounds good to me, but we didn't bring any clothes."

"No problem. There are plenty of my sister's clothes here that'd fit you. My niece's would be a bit big on Alisa, but they'll do."

Uncle Charlie announced that lunch was ready, so Clint led the way to the kitchen.

Wherever Alisa went, Rodeo went, and she constantly reached out to pet him.

"I packed a picnic basket," his uncle said. "Why don't you and Susan have a picnic up on the hill. If Alisa would like, we could eat and then read a book. How about that, Alisa?"

Alisa grinned. "And have an ice-cream cone?"

Charlie laughed. "I knew you wouldn't forget that."

Clint thought of being alone with Susan on a

blanket in the shade of the lodgepole pines on the hill. They could share more than just chili.

"Two picnics in two days?" Susan said. "That's more than I've been on in my entire life, unless you count restaurants with sidewalk seating."

"Nope. Doesn't count," Clint said. "My, you're changing into a country gal right before my eyes. Pretty soon, I'll have you roping and yodeling."

Clint whistled as he slipped his hand into Susan's. They left the house and walked up the hill. He felt happy, alive, and he suspected it was due to being alone with Susan.

Susan shook out the blanket and let it drift to the ground. She looked around, smiling. She was noticing the beauty of his ranch. His cattle were grazing on the silvery green grass in the distance, and the horses were doing the same up on the hill to their left. The pond glittered in the distance.

He never realized it, but he missed the Lazy S. Or maybe he was just seeing it again through her eyes.

It surprised him that Susan was so calm and quiet and observant. He half expected her to whip out a laptop or that overstuffed planner of hers. Her newfound serenity was sexy, and it made him forget about food. He was content to follow her gaze until she arched an eyebrow at him.

"Hungry?" he asked.

"Definitely."

He opened the picnic basket and handed her a wide-mouth thermos.

"Uncle Charlie's famous chili."

He pulled out some slices of sourdough bread wrapped in foil, a bottle of merlot and two wine-glasses.

Susan watched as Clint opened the bottle of wine. She liked how his hands moved and remembered how he had stroked her breasts—teasing, touching, tempting.

She wiped the moisture that suddenly appeared on her upper lip. "So, what was it like growing up here?"

"It was hard work, but there was also a lot of fun and laughs. We'd race our horses in the field. We'd swim in the pond. We'd think of tricks to play on the cowboys. In the winter, we'd be up at the crack of dawn mucking stalls and tossing out hay for the cattle. We'd play in the snow. Snowshoe and ski all over the place. Then there was school, sports and studying."

"Were you a close family?" Susan asked.

"Uh-huh. We still are, even though we're all over the States now. If ever I needed them, all I'd have to do is pick up the phone and they'd all come running."

"That's a wonderful thing. You don't know how lucky you are." She looked over at the horses in the corral that were content to stand in the shade and swish their tails. "I have no one to call."

He shook his head. "I'm sorry."

"You think I'm pretty pathetic, don't you?" she asked, not wanting his pity.

"I think you're *wonderful.* You've worked hard to make your company a success. You did it all alone, too."

"My employees are the best."

"You're their leader. *They* followed *you.* Give yourself some credit."

His words made her heart soar. She needed to hear that.

Yet, what had it cost her?

"So in all the years there you've never been married?"

"No. When I was dating and made it clear that my business came first, men made their excuses and never called again. A couple of the men I've dated actually tried to woo me in an attempt to take over my business." She looked at him. "How did *you* do it, Clint? You have a successful operation here from what I can tell, yet you're calm and cool and can do what you want. What's your secret?"

He laughed. "I have great people who work for me, so I leave them to do what they're good at—just what I advised you to do when you first got here."

She'd been mulling that over from time to time. She supposed it was good advice, but she couldn't embrace the concept yet. It was *her* company. She started it and no one could do as good a job as she could. No one cared about the business like she did.

"Tell me the truth," she asked. "Why did you keep the Lazy S when your parents didn't want it?"

He pushed back his hat with a thumb. "I had hoped to settle down with Mary Alice Bonner. I'd dated her through most of high school, and asked her to marry me. When that didn't work out, I guess I just wanted a place to come back to, and this was the only home I knew."

She smiled. "Your home on the range?"

He raised his eyebrows, looking surprised that she got the connection.

"You sing, whistle or hum that song several times a day. Now I know why. But you're not here much, are you?"

"No. But I know it's here whenever I'm ready to…"

"To what?" she pressed.

"To hang up my spurs. It's a cowboy expression," he explained, probably when he saw the baffled look on her face.

"You mean, settle down? Give up bullfighting?" She took another sip of wine and stared up at the clouds. "I can't imagine retiring from Winners Wear. Not in a million years."

He seemed disappointed when she said that. "Yeah, well…me, neither, but bullfighting is a young man's sport. I'm getting past my prime."

He looked fabulously prime to her. Just like he had last night.

"Clint, I want to thank you for last night. I knew that…well…that you had other things on your mind. We both did."

Her smile was shy, and he wanted to kiss her luscious lips.

"But being with Alisa all day, and then seeing that picture of Elaine, I guess I had a meltdown. And you're just so easy to talk to. I've never told anyone what I told you."

He shrugged. "You needed to talk. Glad I was there."

"You'll never know how much you helped. How much last night meant to me."

She moved closer and kissed him on the cheek.

"Mmm…nice." He put his arm around her and listened to the birds chirp, smelled the fresh air and thought that he'd never felt more content.

"Susan, I hope that someday, you'll realize that you just couldn't protect your sister, and that it wasn't your fault. Elaine knew you loved her and you did your best."

"I know that now." Tears pooled in her violet eyes, yet she smiled. "You helped me figure it all out, Clint."

He took her hand again and kissed the back of it. "You know that your mother wasn't right in laying all that responsibility on you, don't you?"

His arm reached around to her shoulder, and he hugged her to his side. She let her head rest in the crook of his shoulder, and she took a deep, calming breath.

"I guess I always knew that, but it was hard to accept that my mother could be wrong. She knew everything."

"Maybe she didn't after all, huh?"

"Maybe not," Susan conceded. "But she was so strong, so fiercely independent."

Clint raised an eyebrow. "Like you?"

She didn't answer that, but she knew what he left unsaid. Sometimes, she thought now, being strong and fiercely independent wasn't a good thing. It didn't mean being isolated and handling everything on your own. Everyone needed help.

Clint was making her see that. He had released

another thing out of that locked box inside her heart. Maybe it wasn't laid to rest yet, but it was out.

The worst still remained.

Chapter Twelve

"I can't believe that I'm just sitting here outside and talking." Susan raised her hands. "I haven't even felt the need to call Bev. Wonder what's wrong with me?"

"Maybe it's called relaxing," Clint said.

"I don't even know the meaning of that word— although I am feeling the need to plan more for my classes. They start tomorrow, you know. I had Bev send me some notions and T-shirts from Winners Wear. When I see what's there, I think I'll be okay," Susan said, eating the last spoonful of Uncle Charlie's chili. "That was delicious chili."

"He'll love to hear that."

Susan took a deep breath and let it out. "So this is how relaxing feels." She slipped her sandals off and felt the cool grass under her feet, something she'd never be able to do in New York.

"I can't believe you don't spend more time here." Susan looked around at the rolling land. "It's just magnificent. All this land. And no neighbors as far as the eye can see. Everything is just like a picture."

"I do like the quiet," he said. "There might be no neighbors, but there's about a dozen down-on-their-luck cowboys who live in the bunkhouse and in a couple of shacks on the other side of the barn. They wander in by word of mouth, or I find them and send them to Uncle Charlie. They heal if they are injured from rodeo or bull riding. When they're able, they'll pay back by working, then they go on their way."

"So you take in stray cowboys?"

"I guess that's one way to put it."

"You're amazing."

He chuckled. "That's what all the women say."

She raised an eyebrow, tried to hide a grin. She knew he was joking, but she didn't doubt that he was an experienced lover. Her stomach fluttered at the thought, and her mouth went dry. She held out her glass for another refill of wine.

Clint uncorked the bottle and filled her glass. "So you like it here?"

"Very much."

"Do you think Alisa likes the Lazy S?" he asked.

"What kid wouldn't? Horses and ponies, a dog that never leaves her side, killer bulls on the hill, a built-in pool—it's pure heaven. Why do you ask? Thinking of taking in stray orphans?"

She was kidding him, but he wasn't smiling. He turned serious.

"You know I like her. Maybe, if she's not adopted right away, she could come and visit," he said. "Maybe she could stay all summer."

"And you'd leave her with Uncle Charlie while you're bullfighting and towing your trailer from rodeo to rodeo? She'd be lonely, Clint. She wants you, and you know it."

He looked into the wineglass as if the answer would be written there in the merlot.

She reached for his hand and held it. "You know, Clint, I waited all my life for my father to come back from his trips. When he was home, I could almost pretend that we were a family, but something was always missing—his commitment to us, I guess. Elaine and I wanted a father. I know Uncle Charlie is here, but Alisa needs you, Clint. All of you—your heart, your love—all of it."

He took a big gulp of wine. "I know. I can't adopt her."

"Were we even talking about adopting?" Susan asked, confused.

"No, I guess not. I just know she's special to me—she's not just another camper."

"Me, too. But neither one of us has the lifestyle to raise a child. Could you change for her, Clint? Could you give up your trailer and live at your ranch for her?"

Clint swore under his breath.

Hand in hand they walked back to the ranch house.

When they got inside, Clint headed for the kitchen to empty the picnic basket and Susan followed. She went over to the sliding door and saw Alisa sleeping on a lounge chair under an umbrella and Uncle Charlie reading a book.

"She's still sleeping," Susan told Clint. "Poor thing must be exhausted."

"She's had an exciting day."

Clint slid the door open, and they walked down the stairs to the concrete patio.

Susan started to pull out a chair from a round table with a purple umbrella, but Uncle Charlie got up and motioned for them both to follow him. He picked a spot away from the sleeping Alisa.

"Clint, why don't you take Susan on a trail ride? Show her the pond and the upper pastures and the cattle. I'm all right here with the little girl.

I'm enjoying her company, even though she fell asleep during *Harry Potter.* Can you imagine that?"

His eyes were the same color as Clint's and glittered with amusement.

Uncle Charlie herded them toward the patio door. "She'll be okay. We'll go back to reading Harry."

Clint turned to Susan. "How about it?"

The expression on his face was strangely intense, as if he were thinking about more than a horse ride.

"Let's go," she said.

They were both in the kitchen when Clint whispered in her ear, "Wait a minute. Something's going on. I can tell how my uncle is acting." He led her toward the window over the sink, where they had a perfect view of the backyard.

Clint stood behind her. She could feel the warmth of his breath. All she had to do was turn around...

Alisa lifted her head from the lounge chair and grinned at Uncle Charlie. "Are they gone?"

"Yep. Trail ride to the pond, just like we planned. Just between us, Susan is only the second gal that Clint ever brought home. I think she's special to him."

"Oh, cool. Do you think they'll kiss?"

"Maybe." Uncle Charlie cleared his throat and began reading.

* * *

Clint looked at Susan as they headed for the barn. "Seems like we have a couple of matchmakers on our hands, along with Emily Dixon."

"Emily?"

"Emily and Dex have had a couple of successes. Jake and Beth are their biggest coup to date."

"But the two of *us,* Clint?"

"Is it so strange? The CEO and the clown?"

"Bullfighter. You said you wanted to be called a bullfighter." It seemed natural to slip her hand into his. "Well, don't you think it's strange? I mean, we don't have anything in common."

When he stopped and looked at her, it seemed like he could see right through to her very heart. She couldn't move, couldn't exhale, she just waited and wondered what he was thinking, what he was going to do.

He swore under his breath, pulled her toward him and crushed her to his chest. His lips moved on hers, and she felt power surging inside him. She held on to his shoulders to steady herself and could feel his muscles tighten. His tongue traced her lips and she opened for him. Their tongues met in a fierce dance.

He pulled away. "Susan?" he whispered.

She knew what he was trying to ask her. She wanted him, too. Every nerve in her body pulsed with liquid heat.

"Yes," she answered.

He grabbed her hand, and they just about raced to the barn. Clint slid the door open, shutting it behind them and then locking it with a metal latch.

"Tell me that you don't want strings," he said. "No commitment."

In that moment, Susan realized while that might have been true at one time, it wasn't now. She wanted much, much more from him. She wanted him to be a friend, a lover. She wanted to know everything about him. But it was all so impossible. He had his life, and she had hers, and they were thousands of miles apart, not only in geographical distance, but also in the way they lived and worked.

But she'd take the memory of what it was like to be with him back to New York and treasure it always.

Her heart pounded so loudly she was sure he could hear it. She was about to lie to him, and she'd never lied in her life.

"No strings," she finally said.

He took his hat off and hung it on a nail protruding from a thick wooden beam.

Tugging on a blanket that was folded over a stall, he tossed it onto the hay. Taking Susan with him, he fell onto the blanket.

"Take off your blouse," he whispered. "I want to see you. All of you."

She could see the sun streaming through the dusty windows, illuminating them both in golden light. Vaguely she heard the moving of horses in the stalls. She could see a tiny scar on Clint's chin, the little indentation on the side of his mouth. She could smell the scent of the earthy barn and the sweetness of the hay.

It reminded her of the barn at the Gold Buckle, the barn where he'd swept her into his arms and danced with her. She'd bared some of her soul to him there.

There'd be no dancing now.

"You first," she whispered, suddenly nervous.

He knelt and shrugged off his shirt. She saw his scars, the scars from his dangerous job. A job he could lose his life while doing. That was another reason why she couldn't give her heart to him. She might lose him.

Without taking his eyes off of her, he yanked on his belt buckle, loosened his belt and pulled off his boots. He popped the button on his jeans, then started on the zipper.

A fog settled on Clint's brain. He couldn't think for the life of him.

Susan deserved slow and passionate lovemaking, but he was on fire. He'd never wanted a woman so much in his life.

He watched as she undid the buttons on her blouse, tossing it next to his shirt on the hay. She wore a sexy, lacy white bra with a front closure.

"Don't touch that," he ordered. He wanted to unhook it himself.

She smiled and slipped out of her shorts and adjusted the little flowered bikini underwear that she wore.

Looking up at him, she pointed to his jeans. "Take them off. I want to see you, too."

He pulled his jeans off. No sexy underwear for him, just white briefs that were feeling suddenly too small.

He fisted his hands on the front of her bra and unhooked it. Her breasts sprang free, her silken skin stark white against his tanned hands.

He touched, stroked and nibbled, then trailed kisses over her breasts. He teased her nipples with his teeth and tongue. He could taste the wine on her lips, smell the perfume on her skin, and feel her nails on his back.

He stopped himself from tearing off her panties, trying to take it slow, but with Susan he was once again a horny high school junior in the front seat of his pickup.

Finally, they were naked, skin to skin, mouth to mouth. She whispered his name and reached for him. She ran her soft hand up and down his length, until he thought he'd explode. When she squeezed him, he knew he would.

He couldn't reach his jeans, couldn't get to his wallet. He swore.

"Clint?"

He winked. "Don't go anywhere."

Her eyes twinkled. "As if I could." Her voice was low, sexy.

With a grunt, he moved off her, grabbed his jeans, found his wallet. He pulled out a condom and tore a corner out of the packet with his teeth.

Watching Clint unroll the condom over his arousal had to be one of the sexiest things Susan had ever seen. He was hard and long, and breathtakingly masculine.

At least he had enough sense to use protection—she'd never even thought of it.

"You're gorgeous, Clint."

He grinned and pulled her on top of him.

Her tongue made circles on his nipples as her hands explored his chest and stomach.

He cupped her breasts in his hands, his thumbs pressing on her nipples. They peaked under his touch and the warmth of his tongue. She lost all sanity. All she could think of was feeling him move inside her. She wanted him more than ever.

She met his gaze and positioned herself over

him. Slowly, she took the length of him inside her, giving herself time to adjust to his width.

He filled her completely, totally. She couldn't move; all she could do was gaze into his eyes. Then she rode him, slowly at first, then faster.

"Susan." His voice didn't sound like his when he whispered her name. "Stop moving or things are going to be over sooner than I'd like."

He rolled over, taking her with him, wincing to hold himself in check.

His tongue demonstrated what he was going to do to her, and she could feel her muscles constrict and throb around him. She moved her hips to take more of him, and he buried himself deep inside her.

They moved together as two parts of one whole, faster and faster until they were both sweaty and spent.

Holding on tight, they drifted back to reality, back to Clint's barn at the Lazy S.

They could only look into each other's eyes and smile as their pulses returned to normal.

Clint kissed her forehead, let his lips linger on hers.

She already regretted their agreement. She could hardly tell him that she'd just had the best experience of her life.

Or that she thought she was falling in love with him.

She'd just given her everything to him. Her heart was lying like a lump in her chest as she thought about how her days in Wyoming were coming to an end. Then Clint would go one way, and she'd go another.

That's just what she was afraid of, losing the people she cared for and missing them every day of her life.

But she'd throw herself into her work, like she always had, and the pain would dull in time.

Chapter Thirteen

Instead of taking the horses, Clint drove Susan out to the pond on an electric golf cart. He made up some lame excuse about how it was time for the horses to eat.

Actually, he just wanted to sit with his arm around her. What they'd just shared in the barn rocked him to the soles of his boots.

Her mere touch inflamed him like nothing—or no one—ever had. They had fit together so perfectly, and when she met her release...hell, it made *him* feel good just watching her face.

She was nothing like the woman who'd stepped off the plane at the Mountain Springs Airport a few days ago. That woman was a top spinning out of control. The new Susan Collins was calmer, more aware of her surroundings, more appreciative of the beauty of nature.

Just watching her face, flushed with animation and wonder and a hint of a tan, made him feel good that he'd played a part in getting her to slow down.

He'd also take some of the credit for that glow on her face.

He'd never felt as close to any other woman as he did to Susan, not even Mary Alice.

Who would have thought that Clint Scully would fall for a city slicker?

"It's so beautiful here." She pointed ahead. "Clint, what are all those?"

He looked to see a small herd drinking at the water's edge. "Elk." He cut the motor so they wouldn't run off.

"So many of them? Oh, and look at the babies."

"You've never seen elk before?"

"It's not as if they roam around Manhattan and drink out of the fountains, cowboy."

"True."

"Alisa will be disappointed that she missed this."

"She's probably having a ball singing tunes from *The Little Mermaid* to Uncle Charlie."

"That reminds me, I'm going to talk to Emily

when I get back. I'd like to pay for Alisa's operation and any expenses. I want her to go to the best hospital and have the best surgeon available, not someplace that Children's Services will send her. Emily said that her operation would be at the end of the summer. I think she should have it done in New York. I have connections at some of the top hospitals there."

"And who's going to visit her or take care of her way over in New York City? You?" He raised an eyebrow. "Won't you be busy at your company?"

Her eyes widened. Obviously she hadn't gotten that far in her thinking yet.

"I'm assuming her adoptive parents will be with her," she replied.

"And you'll supply the money for them to travel with her?"

"Yes. If they need it."

"And that will make you feel better?" Clint asked, not making eye contact. "By throwing money in her direction, you don't have to get further involved."

"But there's nothing else I…we…can do for her."

"That's not true, and you know it."

He started up the golf cart and headed left around the lake. The elk scattered.

"You wouldn't visit Alisa in the hospital?" he asked. "She'd be crushed."

"Of course I would."

"If you can fit her into your schedule, that is."

"I'll block out time," she said.

"You'll *block out* time?" he said sarcastically. "Isn't that considerate of you?"

"Clint, what's your problem?"

He swung the cart away from the lake. He didn't know why he was so perturbed. It was very nice of Susan to provide Alisa the best medical attention that money could buy, but she still wasn't able to get personally involved with Alisa. She was still comparing her to Elaine.

He'd thought she was over that.

Alisa needed Susan. The girl adored her, and if Susan would let herself, she'd see that she needed Alisa, too.

"Are you scared to go to the hospital because you'd be living Elaine's illness all over again through Alisa?"

"I don't know. Maybe." She looked down at her hands, which were so tightly entwined on her lap that her knuckles were white. "I know that Alisa's condition isn't terminal, and logically, I should stop being such an idiot."

She had such a pained look on her face that he knew she was struggling with her decision.

"Alisa needs you, Susan. You're terrific with her. You know she adores you."

"She adores you, too, Clint."

"That's why I'm going to be there for her, no matter where her operation is. And what do I tell her when she asks for you? That you are too busy?"

"I don't want her to think that." She shook her head. "I just need time to figure things out. To digest everything. I need time to think about my life— past, present and future." She met his gaze. "And *that* is something that I never thought I'd say. I've always tried to stick to reaching my professional goals. I'm detouring into unfamiliar territory here."

Who was he to sit in judgment of her? She'd work through it. She was almost there. He had his own hang-ups. He had a ranch he didn't work. He lived in a trailer that he towed around the country with a beat-up truck. If it weren't for Cletus the Clown and Joe Watley, he'd be broke. If it weren't for Uncle Charlie, he wouldn't have a successful ranch.

His time with Susan and Alisa made him realize that he had the hearth and home, but he wanted a family of his own. That's why he worked with the Wheelchair Rodeo and the Gold Buckle Gang, and visited hospitals. He liked to think of those kids as his own. They were the ones who needed him—kids like Alisa.

He'd like his own kids, too, to ride all over his ranch, to swim in the pond, to play tricks on the ranch hands, just like he had. A baker's dozen ought to do.

Yes. This was what he'd always wanted.

He looked at the woman sitting beside him. Susan certainly didn't share his dreams, and that left a hollow feeling inside him.

Sure, they had great sex in the barn a while ago, but that was just slaking their mutual lust. Wasn't it?

Susan broke the silence. "What happened to Mary Alice Bonner?"

"That came out of nowhere."

"I know. But I was just wondering what happened."

"She left me at the altar, ran off to do her thing in Chicago. She wanted to design her own jewelry. She made a big success out of it, too, and I never heard from her again."

"That must have hurt you."

"Like being gored by a bull. I mean, she could have told me earlier. Or in person." He shrugged. "But that's old news. It was a couple of years ago."

There had been many eager buckle bunnies in his career, but that was only sex. That's all he'd let himself want.

Until now.

Now he could picture Susan and Alisa on his ranch, riding horses, laughing, swimming in the pool and pond.

But he couldn't get his hopes up like that.

No commitment.

Yes. No. Yes. No. He was driving himself crazy.

Clint cleared his throat. "Let's go see what Alisa and Charlie are up to."

Susan dove into the pool, grateful for the cool, clear water. She came up for air near where Alisa floated on a small pink tube.

"Hi," Alisa said. "Did you go on a horse ride?"

Susan stood and moved a wet strand of Alisa's hair behind her ear. "Clint said the horses had to eat supper, so we went for a ride in a golf cart instead."

A memory of their afternoon in the barn flashed through her mind, and Susan ducked under water to cool her heated cheeks.

Clint came out wearing cutoff jeans. He hit the diving board, splashing them both with a well-placed cannonball.

After they both splashed Clint in retaliation, Susan found a floating lounge chair and leaned back to watch the two of them play in the water.

Clint held Alisa in his arms and swung her around in the water. They played with a beach ball, played ring toss, and Clint gave Alisa yet another piggyback ride.

Maybe he'd bought the ranch back to give to

his parents, but he'd kept it for Mary Alice Bonner and himself.

She looked at him in a new light. He wasn't just a tumbleweed traveling in his trailer. The Lazy S was what Clint longed for. He'd remodeled his home, added his own touches to it, and if Mary Alice hadn't left him, he'd be here with her now.

She looked at him, stunned by what she'd concluded. Clint was strong and sweet, masculine and yet sensitive. He was great with kids. She marveled at how he was playing with Alisa and listening to her chatter.

Clint would make a wonderful father.

But Clint was no different from her father. He worked the summer programs at the Gold Buckle Ranch, and then he was gone.

He even left his beautiful ranch for others to run, just like her father left her mother to run the household.

Susan said a quick prayer that whoever adopted Alisa would play with her and spend lots of time with her.

Every kid deserved that.

Later, Susan changed into the dry clothes that Clint provided. They settled into pleasant conversation and many laughs around the patio table, filling up on the steaks that Clint barbecued along with a big salad and baked potatoes.

Uncle Charlie started a bonfire as Susan watched the magnificent sunset. Wrapped snugly in the coat that Clint had draped over her shoulders, she could smell his scent lingering on the fabric.

Susan hated the thought of leaving Clint's ranch. She could easily spend more time here with him.

Clint strummed his guitar as Alisa sang her usual songs from Disney movies. When she saw Alisa yawning, Susan called for lights out.

"Time for bed, miss," Susan said, feeling like a mother.

"Aw, one more song. Please?" Alisa begged.

"One more," Susan relented. "But I have a special request if you all don't mind. Clint, will you play 'Home on the Range' for us?"

"With pleasure."

Susan was taken aback when Alisa scrambled onto her lap and leaned her head on her shoulder. Her little hand found hers, and Susan's heart melted. She draped a blanket around Alisa and hugged her close. She could smell the chlorine in her hair, feel her hard metal braces against her own legs, smell the sweetness of melted marshmallows clinging to her.

Susan kissed Alisa's forehead, and Alisa smiled up at her, a beautiful, contented smile.

And in that moment, Susan lost her heart completely.

Clint began to sing. He met her eyes, and it seemed like he was singing right to her. As she listened to his voice drift over his Wyoming land, Susan took great satisfaction in knowing why he loved that song so much.

"We need to talk about Alisa," Susan said to Clint after they'd put the girl to bed.

"I know. Let me take a shower first and I'll meet you in the living room."

"Okay. I'll do the same."

"We could save water and shower together," he said, eyebrow raised.

She shook her head. "Off you go, cowboy."

Susan took a shower and slipped into a T-shirt that Clint had given her.

She didn't wait for him in the living room as they planned. Instead, she gave a slight knock on his bedroom door. "It's me."

"C'mon in."

He swung the door open, and she saw that he had a towel wrapped around his waist. His hair was still wet and uncombed.

Suddenly, she couldn't swallow, couldn't breathe. She wanted him again.

"I want you naked," she said, not aware that she spoke the words out loud.

"Pardon?"

"Naked. You." Susan stood in front of him and reached for the fold of his towel. It dropped to the floor, and he stood in front of her, gloriously naked and not caring a bit. Smiling, he placed his hands on his hips and raised his eyebrows.

"Now what?" he said.

"Bed," she said, finally finding her voice.

He took her in his arms and pinned her on the bed, the hard length of him pressed against her thigh.

"I want to take it slow this time, Susan."

"No way."

He pulled off her shirt and teased her nipple with his teeth. "I thought you were learning to relax and take things easy."

"Next time, Clint. Next time."

She reached between them, closing her hand over his erection. He was already about to explode. He pulled open the drawer to his nightstand, and with a grunt felt around for a condom.

"Let me," she said.

He handed her a packet. With shaking hands, she managed to get it open. She knelt between his legs, kissing the soft tip of his arousal.

Just as she finished unrolling the condom down his hard length, she found herself under him. His mouth covered hers as he entered her. Their rhythm was furious as they thrust together, meeting each other's pace. Susan found release first, and then Clint let himself go.

They clung to each other, arms and limbs tangled. They stayed that way, dozing on and off, until one of them reached for the other to make love again.

Finally, they relaxed, in a state of bliss, content in each other's arms. But as Susan felt Clint's hand stroke her back, she knew that in a few days, she'd have to figure out what she was going to do without him in her life.

Chapter Fourteen

After a big breakfast that Uncle Charlie had ready for them at his cabin, they headed for the plane. This time they had an extra passenger—Rodeo.

As they got closer to Mountain Springs, it started raining, then the weather got progressively worse.

Alisa thought it was "awesome" to see lightning off in the distance, but Clint concentrated on piloting and didn't say much. Rodeo was curled up on the seat next to Alisa with his chin on her lap.

They touched down at the airstrip on Joe Watley's Silver River Ranch at eleven o'clock in the morning, then they took Alisa to the Dixons' home. Clint carried her inside, and commanded Rodeo to stay on the porch.

"It's organized chaos around here because of the rain," Jake Dixon said, shutting the kitchen door. "Glad you're all back. We were all worried about you in this weather."

"Looks like some thunder and lightning is headed this way," Clint said.

Emily appeared in the kitchen, looking harried. "Welcome back." She stared out the window. "The weather service said to expect this for the next three days. It's a mud pit out there." She turned toward Alisa. "Did you have a good time?"

"Cheyenne Clint's ranch is so cool." Alisa grinned up at Clint. He pulled out a kitchen chair for her, and she sat down.

"Excellent," Emily said. "I knew you and Susan would love it there."

"We had to cancel the games, which disappointed the kids to no end," Dex said. "Riding lessons were called off. We've added roping lessons and relay races in the dining hall, and we've scheduled a dance. We're going to need you to play, Clint."

"No problem," Clint said.

"Susan, can you take on more craft classes for

the week since the outdoor activities are canceled?" Jake asked.

She had a moment of panic, and then remembered all the pot holder loops in the cabinet of her classroom. "I can if someone can teach me how to make pot holders."

"I can," Alisa said. "My mommy taught me."

Susan gave her a thumbs-up. "Excellent. You can show me, and we'll teach the classes together."

Her face glowed. "Really? Me?"

"Really. You."

"Joe made a couple of calls and got us the Mountain Springs arena on Friday, free of charge," Jake said. "We're going to have the Gold Buckle Gang Rodeo indoors there. The arena is big enough for two baseball games at the same time. Joe's bringing in some steers for the roundup."

"And then we could do the logo T-shirt competition. I have a little runway fashion show planned," Susan added.

"Excellent," Emily said. "The kids will love it. Then the volunteers can serve hot dogs and hamburgers. It's not going to be as exciting as a trail ride, but we need to improvise."

"I'll help Joe with the stock," Clint said. "We could always bring horses and let the kids ride around the arena."

"Just what I was thinking." Jake gave Clint a slap on the back that would have sent a normal man flying across the room, but Clint didn't budge. "I need to get going. Don't forget lunch in about an hour." Jake bent over and gave Alisa a tweak on the nose, then tipped his hat to Susan. "Thanks for your help, ladies."

"Uh…Mrs. D, we had a stowaway on the plane." Clint opened the kitchen door and Rodeo walked in, looked around, then immediately went to Alisa's side and sat down.

"Rodeo, I haven't seen you in a while." Emily held her hand out, and he walked over to her. She petted him, and when she stopped, he went back to Alisa's side. Her hand automatically went to the dog's head.

"He's taken a real liking to Alisa," Clint said. "He's very protective of her."

"I can see that," Emily replied.

"He can stay in my trailer with me," Clint said.

"Or in the Homesteader Cabin with me," Susan volunteered.

She jumped at the sound of her own voice volunteering to take a dog. She'd never had a dog in her life and would need detailed instructions on what to do, but she liked Rodeo.

Emily's eyes twinkled when she looked at Alisa's face. "He can stay here just as long as

Alisa takes care of him, walks him and feeds him." She tried to look stern but couldn't pull it off.

"I will, Mrs. Dixon. I really will," Alisa promised.

Clint nodded. "I've got some dog food in the truck, Mrs. D. I'll bring it in."

When Susan entered her chilly cabin, she immediately started a fire.

After a long, hot shower, she noticed that she had some aching muscles in places that she never knew could ache. Smiling, she knew it was from her lovemaking with Clint. He could be quite imaginative. Her smile soon faded when she realized that he'd become a part of her life in such a short time. Things would never be the same without him.

She'd never be the same without him.

She'd go on as she usually did. She'd throw herself into her work.

A half hour later, she unlocked the door of her classroom and began opening the boxes from her company. Her staff had done an excellent job in gathering everything she needed.

The last box made Susan grin. They'd packed boots, jeans and shirts in her size along with a denim jacket. She giggled at the pink cowboy hat and turquoise cowboy boots.

She put the hat on and looked at herself in the mirror. Awesome, as Alisa would say.

She'd have to give her administrative staff a raise when she got back. What would she do without them? Then it struck her—she hadn't thought of calling Winners Wear in ages.

Right now, her company was the last thing on her mind. She was more concerned about a little girl, a rodeo bullfighter and helping out the Dixons.

She got everything unpacked, stacked the T-shirts according to size, and put the trim in various baskets and bins. Happy that everything was sufficiently organized, she headed back to her cabin to change into her cowboy clothes.

Wouldn't Clint be surprised?

When Susan Collins walked into the dining hall, Clint Scully did a double take.

It could have been the tight jeans or the pastel plaid shirt. Maybe it was the pink cowboy hat or the turquoise cowboy boots. All he knew was that Susan looked hot.

He was at her side in a heartbeat, and couldn't stop staring at her. He tweaked his hat. "Well, hell-o, Miss Rodeo Queen."

"How do I look?" She turned in a circle.

Clint whispered in her ear, "Hot and sexy."

Her face flushed with heat. "You don't look too bad yourself, cowboy."

"I'd like to make love to you right here and now, but this is a G-rated dining hall."

She grinned. "I take my hat off for only one thing, and it's staying on until lights out."

The next morning, Dex Dixon walked up to the stage in the dining hall and welcomed the Gold Buckle Gang campers. He said a prayer, everyone recited the Pledge of Allegiance and he explained the changes in the program due to the heavy rain and mud. There were groans when he said that the events would be held indoors.

But then there were cheers when he said that there would still be horseback riding and other events at the Mountain Springs arena.

After breakfast, the Gold Buckle Gang program would officially start.

Susan had a nine o'clock arts and crafts class. She could hardly eat or concentrate on her conversation with Clint.

"Clint, I want to go to my classroom and go over my notes."

"Sure. Let's go."

"I've never been so nervous in my life," she

said, walking around the room, straightening the table coverings.

"They're just kids," Clint said. "And here they come."

Her class filed in wearing raincoats, carrying umbrellas and backpacks.

Clint stood at her side. "You can do it."

"I can do it." She drew upon every bit of strength she had in her. "Good afternoon, campers. Welcome to arts and crafts class. Hang up your coats and take a seat. We have a big project to start today."

Susan had the time of her life. She did two more classes and found that Alisa was a great help. Clint provided individual attention to each of the kids.

Even the boys liked the thought of bringing something they made in camp back to their mothers and/or fathers, even if it was only a pot holder.

They were actually interested in the manufacturing process of clothes and asked questions. Naturally, they couldn't wait to start on their logos.

"Tonight, think about something that would represent what the Gold Buckle Ranch means to you, and we'll get started with the designs tomorrow," she instructed.

As the kids filed out to their next activity, Alisa

handed her the pot holder she had made. It was a perfect blue-and-green-striped square.

"I'd like you to have it, Susan."

"Thank you, sweetie. I'll keep it always."

Her light blue eyes lit up. "You will?"

"Absolutely."

"Do you think Cheyenne Clint would like one?"

"I know he would."

"I'll make him one the same color as yours."

Susan walked Alisa back to the Dixons' home after lunch because another couple wanted to meet her.

In Emily's kitchen over milk and cookies, Alisa couldn't have been more gracious, but Susan could tell that she was tired and not up to this again.

Emily took Susan aside. "The Ketchums decided that they wanted someone who isn't facing a hospital stay and rehab."

"I can't believe that they put her through the whole process." Susan sighed. "It's another rejection for Alisa."

"It's apparently the procedure for older children," Emily said calmly.

"What? Trial and error?"

Susan studied the couple sitting on the couch. They were younger than the Ketchums and seemed to be inspecting Alisa as if she were a bug under a microscope. Maybe they were just nervous.

Emily shook her head. "It does seem that there could be a better way, but what can I do? I only have temporary custody of Alisa. Tonight was the only night they could make it this week."

"Another busy couple, I presume."

Emily grunted. "I think you presume right."

Susan looked back at Alisa. At least Rodeo was at her side, keeping her company.

"Good night, Emily."

Susan stepped outside and opened her umbrella. She had no right to criticize anyone's busy schedule.

She'd be just as bad.

Chapter Fifteen

Thursday night, Susan was reading in her cabin when Clint came by with a surprise.

He held up a key. "From Emily. It's the key to the lock on the cover of the hot tub." He grinned. "Emily's still calling it a spa. Shall we try it?"

"But it's raining."

"So? We'll be wet, anyway."

Who could argue with logic like that?

"I'll put my suit on."

"Do you have to?" he asked.

She raised an eyebrow.

"Okay. You're right. Put it on and let's go."

Clint waited for her in the living room while

she pulled a pair of navy-blue yoga pants and a hoodie over her suit.

Clint took the two towels she carried and they walked in the light rain hand in hand to one of the caretaker cabins off to the side of the dining hall. The hot tub was around back on a big wooden deck. Three sets of patio tables with umbrellas and matching chairs were positioned around the tub.

Clint unlocked the padlock and removed the top. Immediately, ghostly fingers of steam reached into the air. He flipped a switch on the side of the cabin, and the water churned into a nice froth.

It looked wonderful.

She slipped out of her clothes and put them on a chair under an overhang, hoping they might stay dry. Clint did the same. He wore a pair of dark-colored nylon jogging shorts.

Clad only in her bathing suit, she shivered in the cold rain and even colder air.

Clint held out his hand and helped her up the steps into the tub.

She took a seat, and he sat next to her.

"This is wonderful," she said, looking up at the black sky. In the glow of the outdoor lights near them, she could see the rain coming down like silver shards. The sensation of the cold rain and steamy, hot water on her skin was better than any spa treatment she'd ever had.

Clint added to the heat of the hot tub when he pulled her onto his lap and kissed her. His hand slipped under the top of her suit and played with her nipples.

"Mmm…"

"I know you like it when I do this," he said, his voice husky.

She clung to him, knowing that their time together would end soon.

She was falling in love with him. She didn't know when it started, but Clint Scully seemed to be keeping his side of their agreement. He hadn't mentioned taking their relationship to a higher level, so she kept silent.

Back at the cabin, they took a warm and soapy shower together, content to feel and touch. They moved slowly, letting the water rain down on them just like it had outside. When Clint finally entered her, they moved as if they were in a sleepy dream, prolonging their joining, not wanting it to end.

They moved to the bedroom and talked in between kisses. Then Clint dozed off, and Susan was content to watch him sleep. She wanted to memorize every scar, every muscle and every strand of hair. She inhaled his scent, looked at the laugh lines around his eyes and remembered how he appeared with the breeze ruffling his hair as he looked over his ranch.

She knew she'd miss him so very much.

Getting out of bed, she slipped into her nightgown and her fuzzy socks. She pulled a blanket around herself and went onto the porch. It had stopped raining after they'd returned from the hot tub, but the leaves and needles of the trees were still dripping rain.

She rocked, listening to the night sounds of the Gold Buckle, sounds that would have sent her scurrying into the cabin and under the covers just a few days ago.

She smelled the damp night air, listened to the crickets or whatever else was chirping, croaking or howling out there.

She'd miss this place. She'd been happy here. It had been a hard journey of self-discovery, but with a little help from a wonderful cowboy and a darling little girl, she'd worked through some things that had been bothering her.

She'd met giving, caring people—volunteers from the community and some chaperones and parents of the campers.

Susan had felt like a part of it all. She taught her classes, and held a fun dress rehearsal for the logo competition in the dining hall.

And she'd fallen in love. How it hurt to admit she loved Clint when they'd agreed to forgo strings. Too bad she hadn't known when she'd made that deal that her heart wasn't a corporation.

She only had one more day here. One day to absorb enough of Clint to last her a lifetime. Saturday morning, she'd be leaving.

When she got back home, she planned on sending cowboy shirts, T-shirts, golf shirts and jackets in a variety of sizes for all the staff and campers at the Gold Buckle Ranch with the new logo. It would be her way of giving back.

She'd also send some terry-cloth robes and big beach towels for Emily's "spa."

The Dixons could sell the shirts to cover some operating expenses or give them away, whatever they wanted. She'd see that they got a hefty supply every year.

She'd even told Dex and Emily and Jake that if they ever needed an arts and crafts instructor during the summer to give her a call. She'd be taking more vacations from now on.

Rocking on the porch of the little cabin, she thought about many things in those early hours of the morning. Above all, how hard it would be to say goodbye.

Alisa must have felt it, too, because she'd barely left Susan's side yesterday. Rodeo must have sensed that Alisa was becoming upset, so he'd tried to be even more attentive to her.

Susan heard Clint walking around the cabin, and soon caught a whiff of coffee. After a while, the door opened and a fully dressed and showered Clint handed her a cup.

He sat down next to her, and they drank their coffee in silence, watching the sunrise together, holding hands, content to be in each other's company.

"I'm looking forward to the rodeo today," she said. "Looks like the sun's finally going to make an appearance."

He set his empty mug down. "I volunteered to help Joe get the stock there. I'd better get going." He gave her a quick kiss.

"I'll be riding on the bus with cabins one and two," she said.

"See you later." He kissed her, kissed her again and ran the back of his knuckles down her cheek and under her jaw. "I'll miss you."

She didn't know if he meant that he'd miss her until they saw each other at the rodeo, or after she'd gone. Either way, she'd miss him desperately, too.

If only things were different.

They sat and cheered for Alisa as she played baseball. She scored two runs, but her team lost.

Later, Susan led Goldie around the arena as Alisa rode. Clint volunteered with the boys.

Every event brought her departure that much closer. She struggled to focus on the children, not her own breaking heart. This was their day.

Susan's T-shirt-logo contest and fashion show had been a success, and the four finalists stood in the middle of the arena. The winner, by vote of several judges, was a freckle-faced boy from Kansas City, Mason Detlin, who drew several smiling faces inside a gold buckle. Under it he lettered "Gold Buckle Ranch" in bright colors and "We Try Our Best."

Susan loved the logo when she first saw it, since it fit the Gold Buckle Ranch's theme perfectly. She'd take the T-shirt back with her and have it duplicated by Connie on the computer. From now on, all the merchandise at the Gold Buckle Ranch would carry that design.

When Clint wasn't needed to help, he sat with Susan and Alisa, bringing snacks and drinks and watching the competition.

He'd miss Susan. He'd make an occasional trip to New York when bullfighting took him to events in the northeast, but it wouldn't be the same. It wouldn't be the magic that he'd found with her here.

Could he give up bullfighting and be content to

stay home and tend to his ranch and his other ventures?

Could he ask Susan to give up her company for him, marry him and move to his ranch? Could he ask her to adopt Alisa with him?

When they had been making out like teenagers in the hot tub, he'd wanted to ask her. Whenever they were lying in bed holding each other, he'd wanted to ask her. He never had.

In many ways, loving Susan was as dangerous as fighting bulls—except any damage done would be to his heart. And he didn't think he could stand it if she said no.

Susan needed tall buildings, public transportation, designer clothes and a cosmopolitan culture. She ran a successful company with a few hundred employees.

How could someone give that up for a quiet life at the Lazy S?

While Alisa would love it, Susan would soon grow bored and unhappy. He couldn't do that to her.

As far as she was concerned, he was just another business deal.

The campers left the Gold Buckle Ranch right after breakfast on Saturday. Susan saw them off into vans and busses as they left for the Mountain

Springs Airport or waved goodbye to them as they drove away with their families. She'd miss the kids, but she had a fistful of addresses and promised to keep in touch.

Emily and Dex came to see her off. She told them that she'd be sending all the merchandise they wanted, free of charge, and they couldn't hug her enough.

Alisa handed her a white gift box tied with a ribbon. "Open it when you get home," she instructed.

Alisa begged to go to the airport with her and Susan couldn't say no, although she would have liked to have said her goodbyes to Alisa at the ranch, and be alone with Clint. She kept wishing he'd tell her that he loved her. It was perplexing that she had no fear in business situations, but she just couldn't get a handle on her relationship with Clint.

Alisa wouldn't let go of her hand. There was no room for Rodeo in the front seat with them, so he sat behind them. Frequently, he'd let out a little whine.

Susan kept glancing at Clint as he drove, still trying to commit every nuance of him to memory. His strong jaw, his tanned hands on the steering wheel, the little smile lines at the corners of his mouth. She could smell his aftershave, the spice-and-pine scent that was all his.

As they pulled into the airport, she knew she couldn't do it. Couldn't walk in and hand over her bags and answer the security questions with Clint and Alisa beside her. That would make it so much more real. She had to get the goodbyes behind her. Then she could dash for the ladies' room and wash the tears from her face before she had to face the reality of walking onto the plane.

As Susan got out of the truck, tears welled up in Alisa's eyes, breaking what was left of Susan's heart. "Do you have to go?" Alisa asked.

She clenched her fists as she waited for Clint to ask her the same thing, maybe look at her and at least gauge her reaction to the question. Instead, he stayed silent, looking forward.

She cupped Alisa's face in her hands. "I do, sweetie. I'll miss you terribly, but I'll see you soon. You're going to have that operation in New York City, and I'll be there to visit you all the time."

Alisa wiped her eyes and pulled something out of her pocket. "I made you another one of these."

A pot holder. Red and yellow. "I'll treasure it always, Alisa. Both of the ones you made me." She kissed her cheek and looked away, hurriedly wiping her eyes so Alisa wouldn't see her crying.

She looked at Clint, and he got out of the truck. Leaning into the truck, he said, "Stay here, Alisa. I'd like to say goodbye to Susan, too."

Susan closed the door and blew a kiss to Alisa. The girl was crying slightly, and Rodeo was whimpering with his head on her leg.

Clint stood with his hands in his pockets, leaning against the back end of his pickup. How could she go the rest of her life without seeing him like this, waiting for her?

Susan plastered a brave smile on her face and walked toward him. "Don't just stand there, cowboy. Kiss me."

Just the right touch, she thought, casual and not needy.

He obliged, long and hard.

She wished the kiss would never end; neither did she want to leave the warm embrace of his arms. "Thanks for a wonderful time. Thanks for listening. Thanks for…everything."

She noticed that his smile wasn't his usual grin, and his turquoise eyes had lost their twinkle.

He wasn't going to ask her to stay, but she knew now that he was going to miss her. Why couldn't he tell her that?

Maybe they'd agreed on no commitments, but admitting that he'd miss her wasn't committing. Maybe she'd read him all wrong.

"I'm going to miss you, cowboy," she finally said.

He took a red bandanna from his pocket and

dabbed at her eyes. Then he picked up her hand, kissed the back of it as he often did, and slid the bandanna into the pocket of her blazer.

"If it works out, I'll bring Alisa to New York City," Clint said.

She waited for him to say more.

"It won't be the same, will it?" he said.

It could be better. It could be forever.

She couldn't stop herself from touching her hand to his cheek, letting it linger there. God, how she'd miss him. They'd keep in touch for Alisa's sake, but it wouldn't be the same.

She clutched the pot holder in one hand, and the white box that Alisa had given her along with her purse. Clint hailed a skycap, shoved some money in his hand. Susan handed him her ticket.

Just as she began to walk away, she heard Clint say, "Susan?"

Her heart raced, hoping that he'd ask her to stay—might even tell her that he loved her. "Yes?"

He stepped back and hooked his thumbs into his belt loops. "Have a good flight."

Her heart dropped. "Bye, Clint."

Then she turned and walked through the door of the Mountain Springs Airport.

Chapter Sixteen

When Susan got back home late Saturday, she took a hot shower and unpacked. She took out the box that Alisa had given her and opened it. Wrapped in white tissue paper was the bird's nest with the three pinecones in it. Tears welled in her eyes as she remembered the day of their picnic at Silver River.

Three pinecones together in a nest: Clint, Alisa and Susan.

Alisa's symbolism wasn't lost on her, either— home and a family.

The phone rang, splitting the quiet. It was probably the office. They knew she was home and thought she was eager to get back to work. Not true. For some reason, she wasn't ready to jump back into the fray just yet.

"Hello?"

"Susan?"

Her heart raced as she recognized that low, deep voice. "Hi, Clint."

"I just wanted to make sure that you got home okay."

"It was a long flight, but I'm here. How's Alisa? How are *you?*"

"She's been pretty gloomy since you left. Even Rodeo can't cheer her up. She misses you." He hesitated. "So do I."

She couldn't swallow over the lump in her throat, couldn't breathe. "I miss you both, too."

"Bet you can't wait to get back to work tomorrow," he said.

"I don't think so. Tomorrow's Sunday."

"Didn't you tell me that you work on Sundays?"

"Not anymore."

"Whoa! Good for you. Are you sure this is the Manhattan tornado that landed in Wyoming ten days ago, or do I have the wrong number?"

Clint could always make her laugh.

"You do not have the wrong number, Cheyenne Clint. I am a changed woman."

"See what a little good sex can do for you?"

It was more than sex—at least for her. Still, her face heated as she remembered the first time they'd made love. "It wasn't just good, it was great. And quit fishing for compliments."

She heard him laugh, then more silence.

"Clint? Are you there?"

"I really miss you. You know that? And you've been gone only eleven hours."

He missed her.

She thought she could settle for seeing him occasionally at the Gold Buckle Ranch, but that wasn't nearly enough. Maybe the three of them could meet somewhere at Christmas.

No. That wasn't enough, either. She wanted to see him every day for the rest of her life, but she'd bargained that away.

"I'll call you tomorrow," Clint said. "Right now, I have to load some stock for Joe. I just wanted to make sure you got home safe. Good night, Susan. Sleep well."

She couldn't wait to talk to him again.

"Give Alisa a hug for me. Say hi to everyone."

"You got it."

She hung up the phone and sat by herself in her apartment. Night had fallen, but she didn't bother to turn on a light. She felt so alone. She missed Alisa singing her Disney songs. She missed Clint's laughter and his company and his touch.

She took inventory of her life. Here in New York she had three friends, an apartment and her business. Those were all good things, but they couldn't compete with what she'd found in Wyoming—family, purpose, love.

She was a different person, and she had Clint to thank. Even if they never saw each other again, she knew that there were some things she needed to change in her life.

She reached for her planner, found the picture of Elaine, and smiled this time, instead of crying. Then she got started on another list.

The most important list of her life.

She worked on her list on Sunday, too, and set up some time frames for completion. In between, she got hold of her lawyer and told him what she was planning to do.

He tried to talk her out of it, but she stood firm. It was what she wanted.

On Monday morning, instead of going to work, Susan went to the cemetery to visit her mother and sister.

She pulled some of the weeds from around the roses and sat on a nearby bench. The sun was shining through the leaves of the big maple overhead, dappling the two graves with shade.

"Mom, Elaine, I can't spend my entire life at Winners Wear anymore. I need some time of my own. You see, I've finally learned that there's more to life than just work. There's also a lot of this world that I haven't seen. So I'm not going to work for my money, I'm going to let my money work for me."

This time she didn't cry when she thought of her sister. She felt a lightness inside her that she hadn't before. Maybe this was the biggest gift she received from Clint. She was able to unlock all her guilt and remember the good times with Elaine.

She sat for a while, enjoying the peace and serenity and just being outside—things she'd learned to treasure.

She arrived at work after one o'clock. After exchanging greetings with everyone, she made her way to her desk. At a quick glance, there was nothing that needed immediate attention, and almost everything was just tagged "For Your Information." Her former response would be to call a meeting and get up to speed on every piece of paper and every minute that she'd missed.

Instead, she pushed the papers aside and pulled out a box of DVDs from the Professional Bull Riders World Finals that she'd bought at the airport.

She unwrapped the plastic and slid the first disk into her computer. She sat back as it booted up. Then she sat upright and turned up the volume when she saw that the beginning introduction was a collage of bull rides—and Clint was one of the bullfighters. She watched him move, remembering when he moved that way with her, catching his smile.

There were six discs, and she watched one every day at the office. She continued to look for Clint, losing herself in seeing him again, reliving particular moments from her week with him. She only stopped when her secretary called her for the third time.

"Janet, can't Bev or Darlene handle it? I'm really busy here."

"Yes, Miss Collins."

She never would have done that before. She smiled as she turned the DVD back on.

The next morning, Bev cornered her in her office. "Okay, spill it," Bev ordered. "You've been awful quiet about your trip to the ranch. And you're not the same Susan Collins who left New York a couple weeks ago. What exactly happened to you in Wyoming?"

Susan sighed. "I want to thank you again from the bottom of my heart for making me go on that trip, Bev. So many things happened to me in those ten days." She walked over to her briefcase and pulled out a stack of papers. "Call everyone in for a meeting, Bev. I just came from my lawyer's office, and I have something important to discuss with all of you."

She crossed another item off her list.

Later that day, her receptionist, Janet, popped her head in. She was smiling, and Janet rarely smiled.

"Miss Collins, you have a visitor, a gentleman who is insisting that he see you. His name is—" She laughed.

Susan stared at the usually stoic Janet. "Yes?"

"Cheyenne Clint Scully."

Susan froze when she heard Clint's voice. He walked through the door looking hot and sexy in his tight, dark blue jeans, a long-sleeved light blue shirt and a white hat with silver conchos. He had on a thick brown leather belt clamped with a big gold buckle that gleamed in the overhead lights. His boots thumped on the old wood floor with each long stride.

Janet stared with her mouth open, and Susan motioned for her to close the door. With a sigh, she did.

Clint tweaked his hat and gave her a smile as big as the Wyoming sky. "So all this is yours?"

Susan couldn't stay put any longer. She ran toward him, needing to feel his arms around her. His embrace was strong, warm. She gave him a big kiss.

He picked her up off the floor and twirled her in a circle without moving his lips from hers.

Clint finally lowered her to the ground but held on to her hands.

He looked so darn good. "Clint, what are you doing here?"

"I flew up with Alisa."

"Oh, no…" Her throat tightened. "Is she okay?"

"She's fine." A finger gently touched her lips. "You sure have a lot of juice with the children's hospital. They moved up her operation a week. I just checked her into the hospital and told her that I was going to get you."

"You left her alone? Oh, Clint, she's all alone?"

He nodded. "Alisa and I had a discussion on the plane. We made a plan. My part of the plan is coming here and talking to you. Her part of the plan is to get well."

He led her over to the conversation pit and sat down. His gaze shifted to the coffee table in front of him. Susan had brought the bird's nest with the three pinecones in it to work. One red and one blue bandanna of his and the pot holders Alisa had made were also on display.

He smiled up at her. His eyes were as turquoise as she remembered. "You've missed us, haven't you?"

"You know I have."

He picked up a porcelain angel that was on the table. "What's this?"

"It's for Alisa. I want her to have it, to watch over her. It was Elaine's."

"Beautiful." He raised an eyebrow. "So you're all set to visit her in the hospital?"

"Of course."

"I knew you'd come through, but there was a time when you wouldn't consider it."

"I know. I've learned a lot from everyone at the Gold Buckle," she said. "I decided that I have a lot to offer the kids and staff. I had a conference call with Jake and Emily last week, and you're looking at the new full-time arts and crafts counselor for next summer."

"Well, I'll be." He pulled her onto his lap and hugged her. "They didn't tell me."

"It's so good to see you, Clint," she whispered. He kissed her forehead, and a warmth flooded her.

"Susan, I have a business proposition for you."

She thought he was kidding, but the look on his face told her that he wasn't. "This sounds serious."

"It is." He removed several pieces of paper from his jeans, unfolded them and spread them on the table. "This is my net worth."

Confused, she didn't even look at the papers. "Why are you showing me all this?"

"I'd like you to take a look."

Shaking her head, she gave a cursory glance at the papers, then *really* looked. She couldn't have been more shocked if Clint Scully had showed up at Winners Wear sporting a three-piece suit and tie.

"This is impressive as hell. You never did give me Cletus the Clown's phone number." She pushed the papers back at him. "I still don't know why you're showing me this."

"I want to buy you out."

"You what?" Her heart raced. What was he saying?

"Call it a friendly takeover. Call it what you want. The money's yours. If you want more for the company, I'll sell some cattle."

She held up a hand to stop him. "Clint, I don't know what to say, other than I'm astonished. Why do you want my company?"

"I don't want it. I want *you,* but if that's what it takes to get you to leave here, the money's all yours. You can start another Winners Wear in Cheyenne."

"Are you asking me to come and live with you in Wyoming?"

"Susan, I'm asking you to marry me."

That was what she wanted to hear, but only if he loved her. He hadn't said that yet.

"To give Alisa a home?"

"Well, yes. She needs us as much as we need her. I want us to be a family, Susan."

He was almost there, but not quite. She loved them both, but she wouldn't marry him just for Alisa.

He got up and looked out the window, facing the towering skyline. Susan knew that Clint didn't belong here, and at this point in her life, she didn't want to be here, either.

She could see the resolve on his face. "But, Susan, if you want to stay here, I think we should find a place to live with a park nearby for Alisa."

"But I thought that the Lazy S was your dream place. You'd move to New York for me?" She couldn't be more surprised.

"I really hoped you'd like the Lazy S. That's why I flew you and Alisa there. We'd be great parents, Susan. I want us to have more children." He grinned. "The Lazy S is a great place to grow up, and a great place for kids to run—and Alisa *will* run."

He knelt down on one knee, took his hat off and put it over his heart. "I love you, Susan Collins. Tell me you'll marry me."

Her heart soared. Finally. *He loved her.*

She pulled his hands to get him to his feet. "What took you so long?"

"Well, we had that stupid agreement, and I didn't think you'd give all this up. That's why I came up with the idea of buying you out. I thought then you could start somewhere else—like on the Lazy S."

She put her hands on her hips. "Clint Scully, you never asked me to stay. I'd give all this up if it meant being with you and Alisa. Matter of fact, that was part of *my* plan—but only if you loved me."

She walked to her desk and picked up a stack of papers. "These papers, all nice and legal, make Winners Wear into a partnership. I'm going to be a silent partner for a while, or maybe forever, but mostly it'll be managed by three of my employees—the three who've been with me from the beginning. We've all just signed the paperwork today."

He raised an eyebrow. "You did all that?"

"If you didn't get here in the near future, I was going to come to you."

He grinned and he held out his arms. "Well, then, what do you say?"

"Well, there's one more thing…." She looked at him. This was going to stab him right in the heart. "Your trailer."

"What about it?"

"Do you think that we could get a motor home instead? If Alisa and I are going to travel with you to bull riding events, we want to travel in style." She opened her top drawer and held up a brochure. "I already have one picked out."

"Yee-haw!" He moved her onto his lap and kissed her.

"Think you could give up being a tumbleweed in order to raise a family, cowboy?"

"In a New York minute. Think you could be a rancher's wife?"

"In a Wyoming minute!"

She stepped into his embrace and looked into his eyes. They reflected his love for her, and she could see a happy life with him full of laughter and fun and music.

"Yes. Yes, I'll marry you. I love you, Clint Scully."

"Finally," he said, kissing her.

"Let's just have a minute alone before we go and ask Alisa if she wants us to be her parents. We'll have a lot to learn and—"

Susan put a finger over his lips. "All we have to do is try our best."

* * * * *

Welcome to cowboy country…

Turn the page for a sneak preview of
TEXAS BABY
by
Kathleen O'Brien
An exciting new title from
Harlequin Superromance for everyone
who loves stories about the West.

Harlequin Superromance—
Where life and love weave together in
emotional and unforgettable ways.

CHAPTER ONE

CHASE TRANSFERRED his gaze to the road and iden-
tified a foreign spot on the horizon. A car. Almost
half a mile away, where the straight, tree-lined
drive met the public road. He could tell it was
coming too fast, but judging the speed of a vehicle
moving straight toward you was tricky.

It wasn't until it was about two hundred yards
away that he realized the driver must be drunk...or
crazy. Or both.

The guy was going maybe sixty. On a private
drive, out here in ranch country, where kids or
horses or tractors or stupid chickens might come
darting out any minute, that was criminal. Chase

straightened from his comfortable slouch and waved his hands.

"Slow down, you fool," he called out. He took the porch steps quickly and began walking fast down the driveway.

The car veered oddly, from one lane to another, then up onto the slight rise of the thick green spring grass. It just barely missed the fence.

"Slow down, damn it!"

He couldn't see the driver, and he didn't recognize this automobile. It was small and old, and couldn't have cost much even when it was new. It was probably white, but now it needed either a wash or a new paint job or both.

"Damn it, what's wrong with you?"

At the last minute, he had to jump away, because the idiot behind the wheel clearly wasn't going to turn to avoid a collision. He couldn't believe it. The car kept coming, finally slowing a little, but it was too late.

Still going about thirty miles an hour, it slammed into the large, white-brick pillar that marked the front boundaries of the house. The pillar wasn't going to give an inch, so the car had to. The front end folded up like a paper fan.

It seemed to take forever for the car to settle, as if the trauma happened in slow motion, reverberating from the front to the back of the car in ripples of destruction. The front windshield suddenly seemed to ice over with lethal bits of glassy frost. Then the side windows exploded.

The front driver's door wrenched open, as if the car wanted to expel its contents. Metal buckled hideously. Small pieces, like hubcaps and mirrors, skipped and ricocheted insanely across the oyster-shell driveway.

Finally, everything was still. Into the silence, a plume of steam shot up like a geyser, smelling of rust and heat. Its snakelike hiss almost smothered the low, agonized moan of the driver.

Chase's anger had disappeared. He didn't feel anything but a dull sense of disbelief. Things like this didn't happen in real life. Not in his life. Maybe the sun had actually put him to sleep....

But he was already kneeling beside the car. The driver was a woman. The frosty glass-ice of the windshield was dotted with small flecks of blood. She must have hit it with her head, because just below her hairline a red liquid was seeping out. He touched it. He tried to wipe it away before it reached her eyebrow, though, of course, that made no sense at all. Her eyes were shut.

Was she conscious? Did he dare move her? Her

dress was covered in glass, and the metal of the car was sticking out lethally in all the wrong places.

Then he remembered, with an intense relief, that every good medical man in the county was here, just behind the house, drinking his champagne. He found his phone and paged Trent.

The woman moaned again.

Alive, then. Thank God for that.

He saw Trent coming toward him, starting out at a lope, but quickly switching to a full run.

"Get Dr. Marchant," Chase called. "Don't bother with 911."

Trent didn't take long to assess the situation. A fraction of a second, and he began pulling out his cell phone and running toward the house.

The yelling seemed to have roused the woman. She opened her eyes. They were blue and clouded with pain and confusion.

"Chase," she said.

His breath stalled. His head pulled back. "What?"

Her only answer was another moan, and he wondered if he had imagined the word. He reached around her and put his arm behind her shoulders. She was tiny. Probably petite by nature, but surely way too thin. He could feel her shoulder blades pushing against her skin, as fragile as the wishbone in a turkey.

She seemed to have passed out, so he put his other arm under her knees and lifted her out. He tried to avoid the jagged metal, but her skirt caught on a piece and the tearing sound seemed to wake her again.

"No," she said. "Please."

"I'm just trying to help," he said. "It's going to be all right."

She seemed profoundly distressed. She wriggled in his arms, and she was so weak, like a broken bird. It made him feel too big and brutish. And intrusive. As if touching her this way, his bare hands against the warm skin behind her knees, were somehow a transgression.

He wished he could be more delicate. But he smelled gasoline, and he knew it wasn't safe to leave her here.

Finally he heard the sound of voices, as guests began to run around the side of the house, alerted by Trent. Dr. Marchant was at the front, racing toward them as if he were forty instead of seventy. Susannah was right behind him, her green dress floating around her trim legs.

"Please," the woman in his arms murmured again. She looked at him, the expression in her blue eyes lost and bewildered. He wondered if she might be on drugs. Hitting her head on the windshield might account for this unfocused, glazed look, but it couldn't explain the crazy driving.

"Please, put me down. Susannah… The wedding…"

Chase's arms tightened instinctively, and he froze in his tracks. She whimpered, and he realized he might be hurting her. "Say that again?"

"The wedding. I have to stop it."

* * * * *

Be sure to look for TEXAS BABY,
available September 11, 2007,
as well as other fantastic Superromance titles
available in September.

Welcome to Cowboy Country...

TEXAS BABY

by *Kathleen O'Brien*

#1441

Chase Clayton doesn't know what to think.
A beautiful stranger has just crashed his
engagement party, demanding that he not
marry because she's pregnant with his baby.
But the kicker is—he's never seen her before.

Look for TEXAS BABY and other fantastic
Superromance titles on sale September 2007.

Available wherever books are sold.

HARLEQUIN
Super Romance

**Where life and love weave together
in emotional and unforgettable ways.**

REQUEST YOUR FREE BOOKS!

2 FREE NOVELS PLUS 2 FREE GIFTS!

Silhouette®

SPECIAL EDITION®

Life, Love and Family!

YES! Please send me 2 FREE Silhouette Special Edition® novels and my 2 FREE gifts. After receiving them, if I don't wish to receive any more books, I can return the shipping statement marked "cancel." If I don't cancel, I will receive 6 brand-new novels every month and be billed just $4.24 per book in the U.S., or $4.99 per book in Canada, plus 25¢ shipping and handling per book and applicable taxes, if any*. That's a savings of at least 15% off the cover price! I understand that accepting the 2 free books and gifts places me under no obligation to buy anything. I can always return a shipment and cancel at any time. Even if I never buy another book from Silhouette, the two free books and gifts are mine to keep forever.

235 SDN EEYU 335 SDN EEY6

Name	(PLEASE PRINT)	
Address		Apt.
City	State/Prov.	Zip/Postal Code

Signature (if under 18, a parent or guardian must sign)

Mail to the Silhouette Reader Service™:
IN U.S.A.: P.O. Box 1867, Buffalo, NY 14240-1867
IN CANADA: P.O. Box 609, Fort Erie, Ontario L2A 5X3

Not valid to current Silhouette Special Edition subscribers.

Want to try two free books from another line?
Call 1-800-873-8635 or visit www.morefreebooks.com.

* Terms and prices subject to change without notice. NY residents add applicable sales tax. Canadian residents will be charged applicable provincial taxes and GST. This offer is limited to one order per household. All orders subject to approval. Credit or debit balances in a customer's account(s) may be offset by any other outstanding balance owed by or to the customer. Please allow 4 to 6 weeks for delivery.

Your Privacy: Silhouette is committed to protecting your privacy. Our Privacy Policy is available online at www.eHarlequin.com or upon request from the Reader Service. From time to time we make our lists of customers available to reputable firms who may have a product or service of interest to you. If you would prefer we not share your name and address, please check here. ☐

SSE07

Bailey DelMonico has finally
gotten her life on track, and is
passionate about her recent career
change. Nothing will stand in the way
of her becoming a doctor...that is,
until she's paired with the sharp-tongued
Dr. Ivan Munro.

Watch the sparks fly in

Doctor in
the House

by *USA TODAY* Bestselling Author
Marie Ferrarella

Available September 2007

Intrigued? Read more at
TheNextNovel.com

COMING NEXT MONTH